MAYBE YOU NEED A MORE
DYNAMIC SYSTEM

COACHING HIGH SCHOOL BASKETBALL

ED HARRIS

authorHOUSE®

AuthorHouse™
1663 Liberty Drive
Bloomington, IN 47403
www.authorhouse.com
Phone: 833-262-8899

Published by AuthorHouse 08/02/2021

ISBN: 978-1-6655-3380-5 (sc)
ISBN: 978-1-6655-3378-2 (hc)
ISBN: 978-1-6655-3379-9 (e)

Library of Congress Control Number: 2021915775

Print information available on the last page.

Any people depicted in stock imagery provided by Getty Images are models,
and such images are being used for illustrative purposes only.
Certain stock imagery © Getty Images.

This book is printed on acid-free paper.

CONTENTS

Chapter 1 It Was the Worst of Years and the Best of Years.......1

Chapter 2 Find Your Yoda 11

Chapter 3 The Importance of
Developing Culture and Climate............................. 27

Chapter 4 Positions, Roles, and Triggers 37

Chapter 5 The Magnificent 7 55

Chapter 6 System Components...73

Chapter 7 Practice to Build Defensive Tenacity
Transition and Speed 93

Chapter 8 Basketball Championship Development............... 115

CHAPTER 1

It Was the Worst of Years and the Best of Years

Billy Blasingame was one of the most terrific coaches I had ever come across. When my editor told me, to write a piece, to kick off the basketball sport season, first person I thought of was Billy. When I told my editor, I was going to write the story about Billy Blasingame, he did not like the idea.

He asked, "Who is Billy Blasingame?"

I said, "Coach Blasingame, is the winningest Girls Basketball Coach in the entire region. The man won more than three hundred games and 12 straight state championships in a row."

"Girls! Did you say girls?"

"Yep Girls. Girls' basketball, is up and coming. This is the "Age of the Woman," in my thinking. Might as well start the season talking about the women's game."

The editor gazed at me for a while then said, "Ok, go ahead, but no one is going to read a story about a man coaching girls' basketball."

The editor turned to walk out. I thought about what he said. Then I realized what I wanted the story to be about is leadership in coaching, leadership in life. My point being very broad, and I thought, forward reaching. That's when I decided to write the article, about men's basketball, to satisfy my editor. I decided also, to write this book, about Coach B. I went to work!

I arranged a meeting with Coach Blasingame. He insisted that if I wanted to interview him, I, let him treat me to lunch, at Hodak's Chicken. I told him that I should be treating him, since he was doing something for me. He asked exactly why I wanted to interview him? I told him about my book idea. He burst out laughing.

He said, "Seriously? Who would want to read about me?"

Hodak's is right off Benton Street, in Soulard, St. Louis, Mo. I had never been there. But I am here to tell, anyone who will listen, I soon discovered, Hodak's has the best fried chicken anywhere. What a treat, to begin what I hoped would be a terrific friendship. I could sense, from the very start, that Coach Blasingame, was just the kind of person, anyone would be happy to meet.

When we met, I almost forgot, as I reached out my hand, to do a handshake. It slipped my mind for a second. Then I thought, "Covid." Jeez, I suddenly remembered, no shaking hands.

I then initiated an elbow bump and said, "Hi Coach. My name is Caleb Armstrong. I'm a reporter. I hope to write a wonderful book about coaching and you are the central character."

"Hi, just call me Coach B. Nice to meet you."

After cordiality, Coach B (He told me during our talk that his players nicknamed him Coach B - I supposed because his name began with two B's - Billy Blasingame), and I began our talk. But

I should say his talk, I just listened and took notes. He did all of the talking. And that's the way I wanted it. I had never met Coach B. I just read the stats one day, while browsing about winning coaches in the state, and was completely taken. The man had legendary type numbers, but that is pretty much where the trail ended.

While interviewing Coach B, I did discover more details. Learned that Coach B's coaching did not start with a bang. Coach B lost his first game, as head coach, 15 to 87. In that first game, his team could not even get the ball across mid-court while the opponent's starters were in the game. Coach B told me that he and his players and fans, were totally embarrassed, and mortified. Coach B shook his head as he revealed that his first team lost six games straight.

As a partial explanation, although not an excuse, Coach B told me, the school, Southeast High School, was brand spanking new. It opened for the first time, at the beginning of the school year. The school district made the rule, that juniors and seniors, living in the new school's attendance zone, could chose to return, to their previous school, or enroll in Southeast High, the new school. Most of the top athletes, in the Southeast attendance zone, chose to remain at the school, they last attended.

Coach B explained that the varsity teams at Southeast were losing in every sport. Most teams had almost none of the Juniors and Seniors, that could have been on the teams. The lower level teams were not, doing as well as they could have either. Some of the more talented sophomores, had been moved to varsity. Consequently, many of the teams, on the lower levels, were left without the players, that probably would have been their starters.

Coach B said he experienced this as an, assistant sophomore team, coach in football. Coach B said he remembered quite well, being in the coach's locker room and office area, after each of the 10 games, the varsity football team lost. After almost every practice, and for sure after every game, the varsity coaches, while talking to each other, were verbally "hammering" the players.

Coach B said that they would say things like, this one can't block, that one can't catch, the other one can't tackle. It was one complaint session after another. Coach B said he privately thought, the coaches were having, "pitiful pity parties." Coach B said he was thinking; didn't at least one of the coaches, ever stop and think, "Maybe It's Me?"

Coach B said, he decided, right after, that 2-18 season, he wanted to be one of the best coaches in the area. He wanted to be the best coach, and teacher, he could be. It became clear to him, he said, that, if he could make, being one of the best coaches, a reality, he had to become a much smarter, and more effective coach.

Coach B told me that he realized that he had to learn more about teaching basketball, skills, tactics, and strategy. He told me his goal was to find knowledgeable coaches who would talk to him about coaching. He was going to dedicate himself to listening and taking notes.

Coach B said that surprisingly, he discovered that he had learned much of what he needed to know, about coaching, from many people in his past. The conversations he was beginning, to remember, had not even been talks about coaching at the time. It all had to do with leadership. Coach B said that he realized he had to become a better leader and he had to teach his players to become better leaders.

The Learning Started in nostalgia

Coach B told me this story. "I thought college would never end! I couldn't wait to get in, was excited to go, and had great fun being there, for the first two years. Since I was having so much fun, the coach had to have, a very stern talk with me. It seems that my fun was interfering with my grades.

All the football players knew, that when a player was summoned to the head coach's office, something bad was about to happen. Assistant coaches' offices, not so bad, but even then, a player was probably still in a little trouble. Terrible thing was, I had already been, to see the assistant coach, twice. So, as I was walking toward the Head Coach's office, I knew I was toast.

Mid-term grades were just out, and I was on probation. My grades had dropped well below 2.0. It was not as easy, to hide those grades from the coach, as it was to dupe my parents. I also had an accomplice back at home.

My little sister, could scavenge through the mail at home, at just the right time (I would alert her as to the time and month in this scheme), and tell her to snatch any letter from the college. Her reward was an outing to the movies, whenever I was home for a weekend. My little sister, a middle schooler (7th grade), was very cool like that (I thought at the time).

After I left Coach Rob's office, I was shocked. He benched me! I could not believe it. Did he forget, I was the starting running back? Did he not realize that I was voted, the most promising running back in the conference, for the upcoming season? The man must be "using drugs" I thought! I was getting ready to go into my junior year, and I had a great spring practice. He could not have missed, those three TD's, I scored in the spring game.

I thought the coach was being way too overreactive. I knew I could pull those grades up, no sweat. It seemed to me that this whole thing was, overblown, ridiculous.

What was even worse was, Coach Rob, CALLED MY PARENTS! This was "off the charts." My parents discovered what had been happening with Monice, my sister; she got grounded. They forced me to attend summer school. No amount of pleading got them to change their minds. Summer school meant no free time over the summer.

I had to be on a deserted campus, in the middle of nowhere, while my buddies and my girlfriend, Madeline, who had promised to love me forever (I did notice that she had been getting "very friendly" with Sam Jones, the basketball player, toward the end of the semester), were back in St. Louis. I, on the other hand, was stuck in Canton, MO. In my thinking this might as well have been Mars.

Another bad thing was, summer school ended on a Friday and football practice started on the following Monday. No Ted Drew's custard, no Imo's Pizza, and most ridiculous of all, no Super Smokers BBQ! This was definitely, cruel and unusual punishment.

At practice, I had to work my way, all the way up, the depth chart again. The freshman kid, from DC, Todd Dempsey, who came in during summer practice, was actually pretty awesome. I heard that he was good. But I never suspected how good. I had to admit the truth to myself. I did not want to admit it, but stats and film do not lie. And in person, he was also a terrific person.

As I looked back, I realized the lesson learned. Take care of business first! My business at the time, was being a good student, a good teammate, and a good reliable friend and person. I was spending way too much time, indulging in the "intoxicants" of life. I was not displaying good character or good leadership at the time. A player with good athleticism, without good leadership, and good character leads to problems. I had to admit, my behavior had become problematic."

Team Camp the First Step

After that first season as head coach, Coach B said he saw a brochure, in the AD's office, from Mizzou's Women's Basketball Program. It was an advertisement for the High School Girls Basketball Summer Camp for teams. Coaches could bring their teams there for a week. The teams would do drills in the morning and play games every evening. Players and coaches would stay overnight.

Coach B said, that was just what the team needed. Coach B said it turned out it was also, just what he needed! Coach B took the whole team. Coach B and the team, spent the whole week, submerged in basketball. During the camp, players below the ninth grade level, were coached by girls, from all over the country, that were MU basketball players. The high school players were coached by terrific high school and college coaches, from all over the state.

Coach B admitted that the camp may have been just as informative for him as it was for the players. After lights out for the campers, the Mizzou players, played pickup games on the main gym court. The coaches, who thought they were still able to play, at that level, were also invited to play. Coach B said he played one game the first night, got whipped, and was smart enough, to just watch, for the rest of the week.

Coach B saw that those D1 college players, were really good. Coach B said that his whole opinion of girls playing basketball, and the skill of the players changed forever, after that week. I sat close to the Mizzou Head Coach, in the bleachers all week, eavesdropping as she talked to her assistant coaches.

The coaches were commenting about the games, and her assessment of players (Lots of incoming Mizzou recruits, were counselors at the camp). Coach B said it was an education all its own. Coach B said he returned to Mizzou summer camp, with his teams, for 10 straight years. Therefore, Coach B was convinced what he learned from coach Rutherford and others at the Mizzou camps, taught him that practice efficiency, leads to an organized and coordinated game performances.

Coach B told me that the skills and strategies he learned at the Mizzou camp were invaluable. He said that he began to develop the system, teams he coached, over the years, would employee.

Coach B told me that there are six components in developing a tough, hard to beat, competitive team. Coach B wanted his teams to be highly assertive, win all the games they should win, and win some of the games, people predict, they will lose. But always, always, always play fiercely, and smartly to the finish.

Coach B felt as if the Mizzou Camp was the catalyst to the changes in his thinking and in his team's play. Coach B said he began to establish what he called, the **six essential components** to the development of highly competitive teams. Listed in order of importance: **Team Expectations, Team Identity, Team System, Triggers and Roles, Position Specifics, and Common Language.**

> "Triggers and Roles? Now that sounds really interesting. I never heard a coach talk about Triggers and Roles before. So, how many Triggers and Roles are there? which of the Triggers and Roles, as you call them, are most important?"

"There are 13 Triggers and multiple Roles, and all of them should be treated as important, if a coach wants his or her team to be really good."

"13 Triggers and multiple Roles, seems like a lot to cover, over limited numbers of practices."

"Yeah, that's why coaches cannot spend too much time, away from the **six essential components.** Coaches have to keep the team and themselves focused."

"Again, which of the 13 Triggers, and the multiple Roles, are most important?"

"The Magnificent 7, as I call them, are the main ones. Those need to be practiced every single day of practice. The other 6 need to be practiced but not necessarily at every practice. It goes something like this, we make a shot - we press then trap, we miss a shot and lose the rebound - we scramble and run a man defense, or zone Defense (this is decided before the game, or at time outs, or halftime). When the opponent makes a shot - we run breaker then offense, when the opponent misses a shot, and we get the rebound - we outlet and fast break, when opponents' cross midcourt on offense - we scramble then trap, when opponents have a take-in under their basket - we do zone defense, and when opponents have side take-in on their offense side - we do man or 23 zone Defense."

I said, "Good grief! That is a lot for players to remember. There are a lot of words used there like, scramble, breaker, trap that you need to explain to me."

"Yes, that is why, I hope this is not, going to be the last time we talk. The rest of the essentials are really important, to drive home, to the players, as well. I think what I am talking about, could be very helpful to many coaches today, and not only basketball coaches."

"So, are you suggesting that the coaches of today are not as good as the coaches in your day."

"Not at all! They don't need me to say it, but most people know, there are some very bright coaches out there. But maybe there are some that are just starting, and can identify with where I am coming from."

I paused for a moment, took another bite of fried chicken and realized that I had eaten way too much chicken, and drank too many sodas (They had free refills on the soda). I felt like I needed to take my notes home, and reflect on what Coach B had told me. I had watched sports for years, but had never heard someone talk about it in terms of Triggers and Roles. I thought that talking with Coach B was going to be eye opening.

"Ok coach B, I think we should make a date for our next talk. I do not want to wear out my welcome."

"Look Man, I could stay here all day talking about coaching." Coach B, shifted in his seat. "I knew you would like the chicken here." He was pointing at the chicken bones on my side of the table.

I smiled as I spoke, "You were right, my friend. This is a great place."

We both laughed and decided to meet again in a week to continue the discussion. As I drove home, I was sure this book, about coaching, needed to be written. Coach B was right, when he said, "It is all about the players." Coach B said many times, "Coaches have to be better, so they can help players be better people."

CHAPTER 2

Find Your Yoda

When I went home, I took out the notes from my talk with Coach B. As I looked through, what he had told me, I became even more curious, as to why he had not already been celebrated, in some way, as a high achiever coach. I went on line to be more creative, in my investigative work. Suddenly, it hit me. There was a big gap in his coaching career.

As I discovered, Coach B coached four years right after college. Within those four years he had a winning, but mediocre record, 47 wins and 33 loses. My research revealed, Coach B, must have quit his teaching job, and joined the US Coast Guard.

When Coach B resurfaced, in civilian life, he was teaching and coaching at several different 1A, 2A, and 3A class, small high schools in Missouri. He circulated mostly in district 6 in each class. Schools like Clopton, Louisiana, Vandalia, Bowling Green, Wright City, and Mexico. Some of those places were a mystery to me. I had never heard of them. He really stayed below the radar. I was interested to learn from him, why he did not coach in the big schools in class 5A and 6A?

Coach B texted me that we should have our second meeting at Rigazzi's Restaurant, 4945 Daggett Ave. in St. Louis. I was not one to visit the city much. I mostly hung out in, what is called, West

County. The address Coach B sent me sounded like somewhere, in the city, and when I looked at the GPS, it showed that Rigazzi's is in an area referred to as "The Hill," in St. Louis.

I heard there were many terrific Italian restaurants on "The Hill," but I had never been there. I guess, like all of us white guys, in my group of friends, the only time we actually went anywhere, outside of West County, was for some kind of sporting event.

We all loved the Cardinals Baseball team of course. We loved the pro football teams too, until they moved. Our group vowed never to even, utter their actual names again (We were harshly punishing them telepathically). One of the teams moved to Arizona, the other has been moving all over the place. Now they are back in Los Angeles again.

I was really glad to see Coach B. We met on the sidewalk in front, gave the Corona Virus elbow bump, then had a seat, in the restaurant. After exchanging pleasantries, while looking over the menu, we ordered; then began the conversation.

Coach B's answer to my starter question was more than I bargained for.

> I asked, "With a record and statistics like yours, why did you, not coach at one of the big class 5A or class 6A, high schools in the state?"

There was a long pause as if Coach B was deciding, if he would answer that question, or maybe how, to answer that question. He looked away, then he looked down, his mood seemed to slowly change to sadness, or at least melancholy. Then he looked straight into my eyes as he answered.

Reflections

"I was one of those "fired up" football coaches. I said everything very loudly, and demanded aggressiveness from the players. I was excited at every practice, getting the players ready for the next game, was one of my positives. It was my style, and it carried over with the girls in basketball.

It was the week we were preparing for Webster Groves. They had one of the best running backs in the area, ranked one of the top three backs in Class 6A. He was a definite blue chip player; big, fast, and powerful. I was certain he would be one of Mizzou's top picks. Some said he could easily end up at Michigan, Nebraska, or Penn State.

Webster's big play was, running him off tackle left, then running him off tackle right. When they were bored with, gaining yards, and running over people that way, they ran him sweep right, then sweep left. You would think he would get tired. However, he was one of the fastest guys in the state in the 100 meters, the 200 meters, and the 400 meters. I was worried about his speed. I feared that if he got outside us, my linebackers definitely could not catch him. Therefore, to prepare, I had the boys work on gaining the pursuit angle, time and time again. We had to contain him.

We had to be ready. I coached the linebackers, so I was in charge of tackling drills. We did tackling drills, every single day, during Webster Groves week. We practiced taking the right approach to make a tackle. We also put an emphasis on leading with the shoulder, keeping faces up, wrapping the arms around, squeezing, and driving the legs through the tackle. I made them do it over, and over again, many reps.

On game day, that Friday night, under the lights, at Webster Groves High School, we came in 6 - 1 and they were 7 - 0. When we arrived, they were not on the field yet, still in the locker room. Our team was already dressed except for helmets and shoulder pads. We all went straight to, the guest locker room, to get ready, to take the field for warmups.

I looked around at the players as the head coach, stepped to the front of the room, and made his final remarks. We took the field and went through our drills. As I was taking the linebackers through tackling drills, one last time, I was hopeful we were ready.

I looked down the field to the opposite end zone. There he was, number 33. I had scouted him twice earlier in the season. He looked much larger than I remembered. I hoped my linebackers could handle his size and power. He was a very difficult runner to bring down.

We won the toss, received the opening kickoff, and proceeded to march right down the field, and we scored! Everyone on the team was jumping up and down and hugging each other. Our fans were ecstatic. We were absolutely fired up! For the first time all week, even though they were ranked #1 in the state, I started thinking, maybe we could actually beat these guys.

The two teams traded touchdowns, a couple of times down the field. We were nip and tuck, back and forth, nose to nose. Then their kicker, missed an extra point. That turned things around. We were ahead by one. It was just at the end of the first half, we had the momentum. But they held us. They bent, but did not break.

They took over on downs, 45 seconds remaining until halftime. The ball was on the 20 yard line. They had 45 seconds to go 80 yards. I felt like we were fairly safe. We expected that they would be passing. But we also knew, their passing game was slight, at best. I was fairly confident that the defense could hold for 45 seconds. I knew our boys, could use the halftime rest break, and the coaches had a bunch of stuff to go over with them.

That is when it happened. It was right in front of me on the sideline. They did not pass! They ran a pitchout to our side of the field. Number 33 burst around his left end. My greatest worry, about this team was happening. 33 was loose down the sideline, I gasped!

But I saw my middle linebacker, Tommy Ross, our most ferocious hitter, coming hard and fast from inside. Tommy had locked in, the pursuit angle. We had worked on that all week. Tommy was on track to blast 33. They were both going full speed, stud on stud.

It happened so fast, I could not do, or say anything to stop it. I saw 33 lower his shoulder. I saw Tommy drop his head, to meet Tyrice Montgomery's shoulder. They were both traveling at full speed. I heard the loud crackle and thud of the pads, as they made contact. It was a violent collision.

It was the kind of hit that stirs the blood of football fans, and excites players. But it's the kind of clash that makes mothers cringe. Our players, on the sideline, and people in the crowd exploded with exhilaration and enthusiasm, over the hit. Coaches came running down the sideline yelling, "Now that's how you play football boys. That's how to hit somebody!"

But there was something not right, as I watched the contact. In my mind, it was like a dream. Everything for a couple of seconds moved as if in slow motion. I was backing away from the sideline as both players hit the ground, out of bounds right at my feet.

The 6'2", 215 pound, Tyrice, hopped right up, shook it off, and trotted back to his side of the field. Our players rushed over to congratulate Tommy, and help him get up. I could see something was wrong. Tommy was not moving.

I told the players to stay back. I believe that they could sense in my voice and body language, something was not right. I yelled for the trainer. All of the coaches circled around. The officials stopped the clock with 5 seconds remaining. There was a hush of the crowd. I saw Tommy's mother running from the stands trying to get to Tommy. The police, at the game, called for an ambulance.

I heard the sirens before I could see the flashing red and yellow lights of the ambulance. I felt sick, I was weak at the knees. My player was down.

When I saw Tommy drop his head just before contact, I knew things would not turn out well for Tommy. I had failed him. All of the time I had spent on practicing tackling, had not been enough.

I overheard the trainers talking with, the EMT first responders. I heard them say, they thought his neck might be broken. I started to softly pray, in a whisper, that no person could hear. All I wanted was for God to hear.

Players and I, visited Tommy and his mother (she was a single mom with three sons, all redheads, just like her, and all football players at different levels), at the hospital, a couple of times in the next week. The EMTs had been right. Tommy's neck was broken. He could have died. Now most of us were worried if he would be able to walk again.

The doctors did great work. Maybe God did hear my prayer. Although Tommy survived. Like all of the coaches and trainers for the team, the doctors were worried, if he would be able, to maintain ambulatory capabilities. Thankfully, Tommy was able to walk gingerly, after a couple of months of rehab. To me, it was like a miracle. I had bad dreams for weeks afterward.

At the end of the season, I decided I was going to give up coaching. I took it as a bad omen, that I received my draft notice, from "Uncle Sam" that summer. I chose to join the Coast Guard for four years, rather than, going Army for two years. I felt I needed some time away. Maybe see a little bit of the world."

Coach B sat quietly as he finished telling the story. He seemed to be deep in thought, almost like a trance.

I finally asked, "Are you ok?"

"Yeah, I'm fine."

"Damn, that was, a hell of a story."

Coach B, called the server over, using fluent Italian. I was totally shocked, sitting there with my chin, bouncing off the table. Coach B, seemed to be exchanging pleasantries. Then it sounded like, he was ordering a couple of beers, one for each of us. Coach B must have said something humorous, because he and the server started laughing. The server walked briskly away toward the bar area.

"Where did you learn to speak Italian like that?"

"Italy."

"You visited Italy?"

"Actually, I lived there for several years."

I just sat there staring. Suddenly, I had a new awareness. I could see that Coach B, was more complex, than I had imagined. I was embarrassed, at what I realize, is my own racism. I had to ask myself why, I was so shocked, Coach B, a black man, spoke Italian? Would I have been as surprised, if it were one of my white "West County" buddies? I mean, ok, I may have been surprised, if it had been one of my West County buddies, but totally for different reasons, and that is my problem.

In a few minutes, the server returned, with our food orders, and another server followed with the beers. The arrival of the food, cleared the air. Coach B began to explain his answer to my question.

Jackson Dupree

"The first week after I finished my four year tour of duty, in the Guard, I inquired about a job, and was offered a teaching position, in my old district. They were sensitive to my past situation as a football coach, so they offered to place me at a different school. I told them I would think about it, and let them know by Monday. Just being in the Human Resource office, at the district, reminded me of

Tommy Ross. More than four years later, I was still in a funk; a four and a half year funk.

My first weekend home, after my discharge, my family invited me to a "Welcome Home" party, in my home town, Louisiana, Mo. about a 90 minute drive from St. Louis. I didn't remember much about my home town. I only lived there until I was five.

When I was five, my father came home, from Johnston Island. For three years, he had been away as part of the secret mission, of the time, to test the anti-ballistic, ballistic missile. He was in the Air Force. Dad was the highest ranking enlisted man on the project. Therefore, he had been entrusted to be in charge, of all the enlisted men on the base.

My dad swooped my mom, and me up, and all three of us moved, to his next duty station, Richards-Gebaur Air Force Base, just outside of Kansas City, Mo. We were there a few years. Afterward, we were transferred, to Ellsworth Air Force Base, about 10 miles from Rapid City, South Dakota. After a few years there, we were transferred, to Italy. We were in Italy, four years. After Italy, we were then transferred to St. Louis where Dad retired. I attended high school there.

At the time, the Air Force was divided into three parts, Tactical, Strategic, and Mechanical. In short, TAC, SAC, and MAC. Dad was in Strategic Air Command. The guys in strategic, did a lot of moving. Dad was in strategic, so he moved a lot, and some of the time, if he thought it safe, he would take Mom and me with him.

Anyway, back to the coaching story.

All week I thought about the offer from my old school district, however, I just could not do it. Maybe it was just my situation with Tommy, and football, or maybe it was simply, that I should just give up coaching. I was not sure why, but I just knew I could not, take the position.

When I arrived at the party in Louisiana, almost the whole family was there. They were so proud of me. It was almost embarrassing. They were reacting as if I had single handedly won the war (Vietnam). They saw me as a returning hero. I did not like all of the attention. I decided I just wanted to live a quiet life, without fanfare.

My family had visited Louisiana, almost every summer, and several assorted weekends throughout the years. So, most of the black people who lived there, knew my parents and knew me. Also, many of the whites there, knew my family.

Once I graduated from college became a teacher, and started coaching, assorted family members, started to really push me to return to Louisiana. They thought it would be wonderful, if I would become a teacher, and coach there. When I was discharged from the Guard, the pressure, to move there, became even more intense.

Louisiana had few black teachers, and no black coaches. My relatives thought that I would be a great role model for the students. They felt that I could be a "terrific" inspiration to both, white and black students.

My mother's brother, Uncle Buddy, was a member of the city council. Uncle Buddy, was the first black person to hold such an office in town. He knew a Social Studies teaching opportunity, was opening, at the high school. It was going to be posted, the following Monday. The Social

Studies teacher had decided, to move back home, to Quincy Illinois, to get married. When the teacher moved, her teaching position became an unexpected opening.

Uncle Buddy said he would recommend me, for the job, to the principal, and the president of the school board. I realized, of course, that Uncle Buddy's recommendation was gold in that town. The whole family was urging me to stay. On Monday I applied for the job. The principal called me for an interview.

I was hired on the spot. I agreed to teach Social Studies and be an assistant basketball, and softball coach. I was purposefully avoiding coaching football.

The next day, I contacted my old school district, back in St. Louis, to turn down the job they had offered. I rented a small, very inexpensive two bedroom, house, on North Carolina Street, in Louisiana; two miles from the high school. I moved my stuff, mainly clothes, into my new home. Surprisingly to me, I was excited to get started coaching again.

That first summer before school actually started, I began coaching softball and basketball summer camps. We held Softball practice in the early morning, then basketball practice in the evening. The Head Coach, Jack Jones, was the head coach for Basketball and Softball. He was also an assistant football coach, and Physical Education teacher.

Coach Jones was young and energetic (23). He was well liked by the players. He was actually from Bowling Green, Mo. a few miles up the highway from Louisiana. He was a three sport letterman in high school; football, basketball, and baseball. He had been a successful football player at Central Missouri State University, a very strong D2 program. He was fun to work with.

I heard, in passing, conversations between parents of players, that Coach Jones' older brother, had recently been named principal, at the high school in Mexico, Mo. The rumor that started circulating, was that Coach Jones would soon leave Louisiana High School, to become the Head Football Coach at Mexico High School.

I learned during our many conversations, that Coach Jones' first love was football. He told me many times; he wanted to be a head football coach. So, it seemed to me, the rumor might be feasible.

At softball practice, I noticed Katy Dupree, a freshman, right away. I discovered later, she was slated to be the starting shortstop, on the varsity. Katy was very quick. She did everything quick and fast, she ran from place to place, had quick movements about her. Katy talked really fast. Sometimes I had to ask, that she repeat things, to make sure, I and everyone else, she was talking to, understood her.

She moved around, as if she was going, to be late for something, or that she needed to hurry, so she could, get on to the next thing, on her agenda more quickly. She was not much for long conversations. She was sturdy looking, about 5'10. She already looked like a senior.

I met him at softball practice. He was at practice every day; always sitting alone. He sat right behind the protective fence and backstop, behind home plate. I discovered later, that he was Katy's grandfather. The parents of the other players gossiped about him sometimes. They said he had been a terrific high school basketball coach, when he lived in Chicago. According to the gossip, he had coached high school and college basketball. He coached many successful years in the Chicago Catholic League, and had retired from coaching basketball, at McKendree College, in Lebanon, Illinois. Some people said he was about 83 years old. He did not look that old to me.

one day before practice, Katy introduced her grandfather and me. As was her style, it was quick."

She said, "Gramps, Coach. Coach, Gramps." Then she hustled off to take batting practice.

"So, from that day forward, he called me Coach, and I called him Gramps.

Katy's Grandfather was her biggest fan, he never missed her games. He rarely even missed a practice. He felt that Katy had real talent as a softball player, but he was certain, that with a little work, Katy could be one of the best point guards in the state. If only he could get her to play basketball again.

Katy rolled her ankle when she was in 7th grade, in the AAU basketball championship game, played in St. Louis. She had to miss most of her 8th grade softball season. To Katy, having to miss softball, was not cool. Katy decided she would give up basketball, so that she could put all her energy into cross country and softball.

I discovered completely by accident, that Gramps' actual name, was Jackson Dupree. Even though I knew his name, we were getting along so well, that I decided to continue to call him Gramps. Gramps did not seem to mind.

Gramps and I became great friends. We often had breakfast and sometimes lunch together at our favorite, of the three restaurants, in town. I paid for the meals almost every time.

Gramps offered to pay several times, but I was running a tab there. I paid my bill, in full, once a month, so it was easy for me to just pay. I loved saying out loud, as we left the restaurant, "Please put it on my tab, Ms. Irma." I would just slip her a five dollar tip, on my way out. I thought I was so cool. I laugh at myself now, when I think back, about that. Gramps must have thought I was such a "dork."

Mid way through the summer, around July 20Th, the rumor came true. Coach Jones, was offered the Head Football Coaching job, at Mexico High School.

When Coach Jones departed, it seemed that everyone in town felt sad and glad. They were glad he got what he wanted; to be Head Football Coach. But sad because he was leaving.

About three weeks later, the principal called me in. He offered me the Head Girls Basketball, and Head Softball coaching jobs. I accepted the jobs, and offered Gramps a job as my assistant on both teams. He took the jobs and that is how we became even greater pals.

Gramps was a wealth of information concerning coaching in general, but also about coaching girls' basketball in particular, he was pretty knowledgeable about softball as well. Gramps taught me things that really uplifted my skill and knowledge base. Gramps told me things that I was able to mold and structure, into my own methods and schemes, that became what I called, the "Yoda Force."

Gramps was my Yoda (A Star Wars, Jedi Knight). Gramps told me that, to be a great coach, a Yoda is needed. Coaches need someone who can coach a coach. For many assistant coaches, the head coach provides that service. Gramps told me that because of this, head coaches are not really good, unless they are teachers first; not only for the players, but for assistants, as well.

Gramps told me things and taught me things, I may have never thought of on my own, or at least it would have taken me, far longer to discover without him. Remembering my pre military, and pre Yoda coaching days, I was so embarrassed, even in my fourth year, when I quit coaching after my best record. I could have been so much better, if I knew then, what I learned from Gramps.

From what Gramps was telling me I formulated my thinking in a way that placed the concept of coaching into three tight modules, Culture & Climate, Skills & Combination Comprehension, Attitude & Resolve. Coaches who want to move from good to great could embrace the components within the three modules, and teach all three simultaneously with enthusiasm."

By the time Coach B and I were finishing our conversation, we had both eaten some great Italian food. We each had drank, a huge glass of famous, Rigazzi's style, schooner of beer. I had recorded many notes, that almost completely filled my new notebook.

I was anxious to get home, to sort and categorize what I had written. I was surprised that Coach B was so forthcoming, with such terrific information about himself and his coaching. I felt like this was going to be a great book, for novice coaches, if I could get it right.

Coach B and I decided we would meet the next Saturday night, at the Mizzou vs. St. Louis University Women's Basketball game, at St. Louis, University. We were both sure that Mizzou would easily prevail, but we thought it would be a fun outing. We figured we could watch basketball, while we talked basketball.

CHAPTER 3

The Importance of Developing Culture and Climate

Coach B started talking, almost as soon as we took our seats, in the fieldhouse. Being in the gym may have gotten his coaching juices flowing. We arrived a little early, so we could see the team's warm-up.

Coach B was convinced, that he could successfully predict the probable winner of an upcoming game, by just watching the warm up. He got really quiet, to concentrate. Although we both, a week ago, had predicted a Mizzou win, Coach B continued to be consumed by watching the warmup.

He seemed to be in deep thought. I wondered if maybe Coach B was missing having a team of his own?

I asked myself, "Did he miss coaching?"

As the crowd grew larger, we could see the clock counting down to start the game. I was looking around at the beautiful structure of the St. Louis University fieldhouse. The place was absolutely gorgeous. I had not been there since all of the new construction.

The place was really starting to look more like an actual college campus. The college had bought land on several connecting streets and architecturally partitioned it off, so that it was starting to look like a university, right in the middle of a city. It was "very cool looking."

> Suddenly, Coach B started talking, "I realized that my attitudes about coaching had changed. Don't get me wrong, I still thought about coaching, and loved the idea of coaching, but there was something different, once I started at Louisiana. I thought I needed to get that old fiery personality back.
>
> I felt I needed to generate some excitement, get the players fired-up, like I use to, when I was coaching football. Maybe that was what I needed. I thought maybe I should get back into football. But then, I met the Dupree's"

Stop Yelling at Us

> Gramps started talking, before I knew the context, "It is almost time for football and cross country to be finished. Time for us to get started. Maybe you could talk to her."
>
> "Talk to who?"
>
> "My granddaughter! Of course."
>
> "Talk to her about what?"
>
> "Playing basketball this season."

I smiled at that comment. Just then, the introduction of the teams began. The Mizzou players looked focused and ready to go. All business. Coach B said he thought the Billikens were too tense. They looked worried.

I was shocked to see Bev McGraw, get introduced as a sophomore starter, for Mizzou.

> "I did not realize that Mizzou had McGraw. I thought she went to South Carolina," I said.

> "Yeah, well, she did. But she got a hardship transfer to Mizzou. Some kind of family issue."

> "I'm supposed to be the reporter here. How did you know about that before I did?"

> Coach B just smiled, "I have connections, my friend."

> "Right; connections."

> "Well, the Billikens better be worried, that McGraw kid, is really good."

> "Yeah, but they did not play her at South Carolina. I think she had some kind of issue with the coach."

> "You have got to be kidding me."

> "Nope. Probably, something dumb too."

I wanted to get back to the story.

> "So, what was your answer, to Gramps about Katy?"

Coach B jumped right back to the story.

> "I told Gramps that I didn't want to push her. That she should make the decision on her own."

> "Really? I thought you saw potential in her."

"I did. But I did not want to be pushy."

"What did Gramps say about that?"

"He simply said, it was silly. He said she just needed some reassurance."

"What did you do?"

"I told her we needed a point guard. I told her she would be good there or at another position. I asked her to come out for the team."

"What did she say? Come on Man, stop being so coy, tell me the story. This is starting to get interesting."

"C'mon, lets watch the game first. There is a pizza shop right across the street, where all the students go after games. You wanna find good pizza? Just follow the students. You can treat me."

"They serve beer?"

"yep."

"You're on."

We watched McGraw put on a clinic. She had a lot of fans at the game. Since she was from St. Louis, a graduate from Pattonville High School. it was an easy drive to the game for fans. The score was already ugly, so by the end of the half, Mizzou's coach pulled the starters.

When we arrived at the pizza shop, after the game, the place was packed. I did not realize how many gorgeous women attended St. Louis University. Coach B told me to calm myself.

"Be careful there Sonny, you are about to strain your neck. You already have an eye problem."

"What eye problem?"

"Your eyes are popping out of your head."

Coach B was cracking himself up laughing.

"All right. Ok, very funny. So, lets order, and get back to the story."

"Now let me see, where did we leave it? Oh yeah, not only did Katy decide to go out for the team, so did the first baseman, third baseman, and center fielder."

I said, "No joke?"

Coach B responded, "No joke."

"Why had they not played basketball before."

"They all had some issue with Coach Jones."

"I thought they all liked him so much."

"I found out completely by accident, what it was all about."

Coach B told the story.

"It was about maybe, the third or fourth week of practice. I was back to the old football ways. I was excited and being very animated in my delivery and approach, with the idea that I was getting the girls really fired up.

But something was not quite right. They were not responding as I had wanted, or expected. Gramps kept shaking his head, as if I was doing something wrong. I thought he was trying to discretely tell me, that I was doing the wrong drill.

The body language of the team was so bad, I stopped practice, and called everyone over to me. The first game after being named Head Coach at Louisiana High, was less than a week away. I needed to discover the problems.

I asked, "What is the matter with you ladies?"

No one responded.

"Please, speak up. I sense something is wrong."

"I looked at Gramps, he looked down, seemingly so as not, to have to make eye contact with me."

Finally, Katy spoke up, "You don't have to yell at us Coach."

"I did not speak right away. I made eye contact with Gramps and he gave an almost undetectable, very slight shoulder shrug, and head nod, as if to agree."

I said, "I am so sorry. I was just trying, to get us fired up."

Katy said, "Yelling does not get us fired up."

Michelle backed-up Katy, "Yeah, yelling does the opposite."

Jana was right with them, "Coach Jones use to do that. We did not like it then either. Seems like you're mad at us, when you yell."

Gramps just stood in back of the group trying to hide, his smile, hidden behind his hand. Not a very good job of concealing it though. Good thing they all had their backs to him.

I said, "I love you guys. I have no reason to be mad or angry with you. I am the complete opposite. I am really proud of you, and the work you all have been putting in. Win or lose you guys are awesome."

After practice and dinner that evening, Gramps showed up at my front door. I grabbed a couple of Cokes. We sat on the front porch and Gramps asked me how practices were going for me. I told Gramps that the yelling thing, caught me by surprise.

Gramps had been talking to me about coaching almost every day since I met him. I just did not realize what was happening. It was not like Gramps just came out and said, "I am going to teach you this or that thing, about coaching." But he just kept up his subtle Mr. Miyagi (from the Karate Kid movies), type lessons; dropping important information, right in my lap, without my noticing.

Just a few days before the "Bull Dogs," of Louisiana High School, would face our first opponent of the season. Gramps told me that things like, the yelling stuff, would not occur, if I would collaborate with the players. He said that the team and I could work together to simplify, clarify, and demystify the culture and climate of the team. He said that everyone on the team, coaches and players, needed to learn, and understand the Team Expectations, and the Team Common Language.

I asked Gramps, "What does Culture and climate for a team mean exactly?"

According to Gramps, "To develop culture, the team must begin with the agreed upon criteria for climate. the values, standards, virtues, and principles of the team as a whole need to be decided."

"How would you accomplish that?" I asked.

"This requires classroom time, with the team and coaches. One of the players could list the words, that come from the brainstorming efforts of the players."

"How would that work, Gramps?"

"Just old fashioned brainstorming. Site the question, that will offer answers concerning team philosophy. For instance, if every player was a perfect person on the team, what would be the Bulldog way? You need one word responses."

"Is that it?"

"No. Every word must be listed. Once all the words are listed, divide them under three topics or categories. Once the categories have been filled using all of the words from the list. The players should be placed in groups of three.

Each group should select, no more than one or two words, from each category, that creates a sentence that would best describe, an average, Louisiana, Girls Basketball, Bulldog's philosophy, and attitude about competitiveness, sportsmanship, and comradery."

I said, "That is a lot of stuff."

"Yes, this exercise alone, could take more than one class session. Once each group has agreed on a sentence, the sentences should be listed on the board. The team should select the best three sentences. From the three sentences, the team as a group, should use the words in the sentences, to make one sentence, on which all could agree."

"That is quite the process. But I could see how that gives the teammates focus, as to team personality."

"Yes, and it makes it pretty understandable, what the team culture is. In other words, the culture is - How things are done on this team. So, what the team and you will have after the process is, the agreed upon philosophies and attitudes that drive everything the team does."

"I don't think, some of the players will see, what this has to do, with playing basketball."

"The Head Coach, does not have to drive everything that happens on the team. It is a matter of fact; The Head Coach should not drive everything that players learn. Encourage them to learn from each other. Have them talk to each other, about what the culture and climate, has to do with them playing basketball. They may surprise the coach and each other. I guarantee, it will make the team stronger and tighter as a group."

The information Gramps taught about the culture and climate of a team is just amazing. I would venture to say, less than forty percent of teams across the country, ever spend a minute, talking about the culture and climate of their teams. Developing culture is really awesome, if a coach thinks about it."

I wondered, but then asked, "Do you think learning about team culture and climate actually helped turn any of your teams around?"

"Absolutely! I was actually doing some of it, but completely by accident. I wish, I had known about it earlier, in my coaching career. But I could say that, about almost everything I learned from Gramps."

Coach B explained.

"I think, having a definite and purposefully designed team, culture and climate, helps individual members of the team, make better decisions. Each player will have some challenges to face, on the team, and in her personal life. Having certain standards by which to live, makes decisions less difficult to consider.

I told Gramps that this whole exercise causes the team to do a lot of soul searching, that could help players on and off the court. Gramps agreed, and acknowledged about the soul searching, but he explained that finding oneself, within the context of team culture and climate, also helps players better learn and understand, the Triggers and Roles."

As a sports reporter, I have really been interested to hear about Triggers and Roles. Over the years, I had not heard coaches talking about that. I was very curious; I was looking forward to Coach B's explanations.

CHAPTER 4

Positions, Roles, and Triggers

I received a text from Coach B. It said to meet him for lunch, at the Bandanna's BBQ restaurant, on 11750 Gravois Rd. He said to be there by twelve. When I arrived at 11:50, he was already waiting, at a table by the window.

I soon discovered that Coach B was a mega "BBQ Hound!" He loved him some BBQ, he really likes the places in Kansas City the best, especially Gates (I on the other hand like Arthur Bryant's best, although Jack Stacks and Joe's are also good). Coach B gave a shout out to Texas BBQ too.

Coach B motioned to me as I entered the door. We greeted each other with the "Corona Virus elbow bump." It was always good to see Coach B. He was one of those kind of people, that seemed to always be in a good mood, with something nice to say, about something or somebody. You never knew what the something nice would be about, maybe a player he saw, have a good game, some random coach, you, or just the weather. I had come to think that Coach B was a "real gem" of a person.

I didn't have to order. Coach B had already ordered for us. He seemed convinced that a person should always order a rack of ribs, fries, collard greens, and baked beans, at a BBQ joint. He said that a person could always take leftovers home. The server brought two, large draft beers, before the food arrived. Of course, we had Budweiser's since we were in St. Louis.

> Coach B said, "To know if a BBQ restaurant is good, several things need to be happening simultaneously; customers have to be able to smell, that wonderful BBQ aroma, at least a block away. If it is a place to tell your friends about, it has to have delicious collard or turnip greens, baked beans, corn on the cob and potato salad, as side order selections, on the menu. If it is a place to take a date, or to take your mama, it must have a variety of sauces, ranging from mild to, "I think somebody just slapped me" hot. Blues music must be playing in the background, over the speakers by day, and if they are really good, a blues band at night."

As soon as the food arrived, and we started eating, Coach B started talking. I was laughing to myself, thinking that the BBQ was like a truth serum for Coach B. I did not even, have to ask a question, he just started talking.

Huey

> When I was in the US Coast Guard, Stationed on Governor's Island NY, I did some coaching as community service. I coached a flag football team and afterward, in the next season I also coached basketball. A game I will always remember, was the flag football championship.

> We were 9-0. It was the last game of the season. We were playing the Warriors, they were 8-1. The one game they lost was against us at 5 games into the season. The Warriors were league champions, in the previous season.

I had bumped heads with the coach of the Warriors all year; especially in the game when we beat them. The Warriors had destroyed the Hawks 45-0, and 66-6 last season, and had beaten them, in every season previous. They showed up expecting to win. They had the "Big Head."

The coach's name was, Henry Phillips, but he insisted that everyone call him "Bear," as in Bear Bryant, famed coach of the Alabama Crimson Tide. He always wore one of those houndstooth hats, at all of the games. I wondered where a person, could even find a hat like that anymore.

Bear, was actually a civilian. He worked in the base bowling alley during the day, and had been the coach of the Warriors for four seasons. He considered himself "famous," because five of his players had made the high school team, on Staten Island, over the years. Only two had made it all the way to the varsity. But it was a big deal, that the five actually made the high school freshman team.

Bear was very loud, always angrily yelling at his players and at the refs. He sounded more like a drill sergeant, than a little league coach. Some of the dads said that Bear, whipped the boys into shape. I thought that he was totally obnoxious.

What was worse, his team was beating us. The score was 25-20, with 25 seconds remaining in the game. We had the ball on the 15 yard line, going in. I signaled for a quarterback keeper, around the left side. There was a really cool reverse pivot of all the backs in the backfield, that we had put in at the last practice, just for this type situation.

This spin by the backs, made it look like the backs were headed to our side of the field. But instead, the play went to the opposite side, then around the end. When Joey, our quarterback, turned up field, he was running full speed ahead. It looked like he was going to score.

The fans for both teams were screaming like crazy. Players on the sideline for both teams were jumping up and down, rooting for their teams. I heard myself saying "Run Joey Run! Go all the way." The clock was ticking 9, 8, 7, 6.

But, out of nowhere, with a good pursuit angle, came the Warrior safety. The safety reached for Joey's flag just as Joey crossed the 4 yard line. But Huey came blasting down the field, and hit the safety with a timely block, just in time.

Joey stepped into the endzone and spiked the ball. He was jumping up and down screaming his head off. The Hawk players and fans were ecstatic.

On the Warrior side of the field, it was the complete opposite. Kids were crying, Moms and Dads looked sad. Every Warrior and Warrior fan, started slowly and sadly, walking toward, the exit area. Everyone except Bear!

Bear went running out onto the field, jumping up and down pointing at the 20 yard line area. He was yelling "Bring it back! Bring it back!" and wildly waving his arms.

Bear was so demonstrative that he knocked his houndstooth hat off his head. It would have been funny, if the moment wasn't so tense. But the sailors, watching the game, as Saturday afternoon entertainment, were cracking up. Then I heard the ref's whistles sounding.

I turned to look up the field and there it was; a red penalty flag. A giant gasping sound, came from almost everyone there. I walked up to the refs to ask about the flag. The Ref following the play, had called a "clip" on Huey.

The roar of cheering, was from the Warrior bench, and fans in the stands this time. The players and fans, on the Hawk side of the field, were totally dejected, as I pleaded our case to the refs. The refs did not relent. The call stood.

The refs marched us back 15 yards, then put 11 seconds on the clock. I called, "Time out." Because of the penalty, we had over twice as far to go; and half the time to get there. As the players circled around me, Huey was completely devastated. His head was hanging and his body language, said what everyone, in "Hawks Nation," was feeling.

Somehow, destiny had robbed us of our undefeated season. We had all worked so hard. We surprised our opponents, early in the season. They were all shocked at our improvement since previous seasons. Some said it was luck, even when we were winning by 30 or 40 points.

When we continued to win, even after they all started "gunning for us," during the second round of games. We finally started to get a little respect. All of the Hawk fans, were so proud of my boys. The Hawks were winners.

We all stood silent. Many understood that our hope to finish undefeated, was probably over for the year. After all, in the seven years of the league, no team had ever finished undefeated. The consolation was that if we lost, the two teams, would be tied at 9-1. Maybe we could win the playoff game. A playoff game had already been scheduled, for the next Saturday, in case we lost.

The team and I were standing right in front of our fans. The fans and the players, knew that our "goose was cooked." But everyone wanted to hear what I had to say. I really did not have a talk planned for this, I just started talking to the players, from my heart.

"Alright Men, yes, we are in a tough spot right now. I know it seems unachievable. I know it might seem to others, who don't know us, that it can't be done. But I believe in you. I know you can do this. These Warriors cannot stop us!

We always keep marching on! When we were down by 10 in the first game, we came back to win by 20; we just kept marching on! We marched on, to win by 22, when Joey was sick for our third game. We marched on, right through the mud and rain, during game 7, to win by 25. And we will keep on marching today.

Some of you might have realized that during the season I always had two plays ready to go at any given moment. The first play, was always designed, to set up the second. So, right now, Men, we have them right where we want them.

Ok, we ran the first play already. Now move in closer Hawks, so no opponent's ears can hear. Linemen, make all of your block's high, helmets up, and keep those fists closed, no holding calls, and keep those feet moving. Jeremy and Sam, let's make sure we seal that defensive end. Pete, go get that safety. Joey, make a safe pitch, make sure it is a toss, that is easy for Huey to catch. You run right beside Huey, protect his flags, until he clears traffic. I looked right at Huey and said with emphasis, "And you will clear traffic! Then run like the wind, Buddy, run like the wind!"

I called the play, Right 26, Huey Special, on 1, on 1.

The whole team said "Ready break!" and everyone, even the fans gave the loudest clap, after a huddle break, I had ever heard. The starters sprinted to the field, with a fury of intensity.

The team ran right onto the field and set-up in formation. The ref blew the whistle. Joey called the cadence. "Ready, Set, Hit!" The ball was snapped, the clock started. Joey caught the center snap, from a shotgun position, and tossed the ball straight out to Huey.

Huey swung wide toward our sideline. He had lots of room, because we had run the ball wide, in the other direction, on the last play. So, we got a great spot by the officials. Just like I had planned. Everyone exploded toward their assignments. I saw Jeremy and Sam, seal the end. Pete came speedily out of the backfield barreling down on the safety. Right behind Pete came Joey and also Huey. Huey was close, but to Joey's outside.

Joey was the second fastest kid on the team, but when Huey got his shoulders turned up field, he just smoked everyone on the field. Huey ran right through the endzone. We won 26 to 25. They did not bother to kick the extra point. The game was over. We were undefeated; 10-0."

Coach B was getting emotional as he told that story. Coach B thought it would help me, understand him better, if he told me about, how his coaching life restarted. Coach B said that as he thought back, what really shook his coaching realization, was when he started coaching the youth team on Governor's Island, New York.

A new friend, Coach B met on base, told Coach B about the youth athletic leagues on the base, and explained that football was going to be starting in the fall. Coach B told me that he looked at it, as a chance to give back, to the community. He saw it as providing a service, by doing some volunteer work. Coach B first thought, maybe he would Ref, a few youth sport games, after work hours.

However, after a conversation with the Athletics officer, Coach B found himself being persuaded, to coach a flag football team called the Hawks. The team was made up of middle school boys. The kids on the base attended school on Staten Island, but because of transportation issues, could not play middle school sports after school.

Therefore, a league was set up, for them, on the base. There were six teams, and each team played the others, two games. Consequently, each team was scheduled to play 10 games. Coach B learned that the Hawks had been the worst team in the league, for the past two years. He told me, he did not realize how exciting, it would be to coach football again. The fact that it was flag football made it even more appealing. That way he would not have to be constantly worried about his past traumatic experience.

Coach B said that he received a list, of the players that had been assigned to the Hawks. he had 12 players assigned. The maximum, by rule, was 15. The Hawks were assigned three more players after a few days. The teams played, seven man flag football.

Coach B explained that his first dilemma was that he did not know the talent or athleticism of the players. All he knew, was the Hawks lost, every game the year before, and the year before that. Those kids had never won a football game, since they had been playing organized football.

Coach B said he felt compelled to do something about that. He decided, he needed to find out, what they thought their positions, on the team should be. So, on the first day of practice, Coach B asked them, to place themselves into one of three groups; backs, receivers, or linemen. If there were players who believed, they should be in more than one group, the player should select his favorite of the three.

Once the players had placed themselves, Coach B put them through what he called, "Discovery Drills." The drills were designed to help the coach, and the players, see where the players fit, in relation to other players on the team. The drills were ones that are, peculiar to the game of football. Everyone on the team had to participate in every drill, no matter player size or age.

According to Coach B, the idea was to see who could accumulate the most points. The scoring was weighted toward speed and power. Players could gain more points, by having speed and power. Other drills could gain a player points, but less points than, those for speed and power.

Coach B explained the drills he used to make assessments about player skills (All players were timed on each event).

- The speed drills consisted of 20 yard backward runs, 10 yards, 20 yards, 30 yards, and 40 yards straight ahead runs.
- Two quickness drills, 30 yard serpentine (Zig Zag) runs, and 10 shuffle runs (two Players stand on a yard line, facing each other, about 5 yards apart, the objective is to touch the lines to either side then back again, a fast as they could, for 10 touches).
- For power, the number of pushups a player could do in 2 minutes, the number of, bent leg sit ups, and pull ups or dips a player could do in 2 minutes for each.

- Another group of drills, Coach B called, "Skill Drills," were used to illustrate, how many catches, on five routes, players could make.
- The players were also required to run 3 square outs, 3 square ins, 3 skinny posts, and 3 fly patterns

Coach B told me that a player gets a mandatory three, attempts, for each event, but players could ask for two more additional attempts if he thinks he can do better.

Points were awarded to each player, such as:

- 10 points for the best performance, in each event
- 5 points, for the second best performance in each event
- 3 points for the third best performance in each event
- 1 point for any performance, below third place, in any event
- Players that received 10 points for the speed portion of the drills received 2 bonus points.
- After the major drills were completed, all players were to compete in a mile run. The players would receive points in order of finish. 15 points for 1st place, then 14 points for 2nd place, then 13 points for 3rd place, and so on.

Best performances were recorded. All best performances were added together, to determine a score, for each player. At the end, of the Discovery Drills, once all of the points were totaled, the kids were shocked that Huey, the quiet, shy kid, who in the beginning, stood with the linemen group, got the highest point total of all the boys.

Coach B sorted for speed first, for skill second, then for power. Players got points in each category. Each player also got a total point count when all three categories were added for each player.

This process gave Coach B a baseline for determining the position where each player would begin. Coach B was flexible, he decided that things could change as the season progressed. Additional information, such as an assessment of a player's toughness, tenacity, or determination could cause players to be elevated.

Players with the highest scores in speed and skill were placed in skill positions. The remaining players were placed as linemen. Players with the 9 highest scores, would definitely be starters, on either offense or defense. The 5 players with points of 10 to 15 on the mile run could be two way players. Players who finished below 10, on the mile run, might not have the endurance, to go "both ways."

Other surprises were revealed, from the Discovery Drills, as well. Along with Huey, who was moved from tackle to running back, Joey was moved from wide receiver to quarterback, and Mack, the slowest kid on the team, who rarely got into games last year, was moved from benchwarmer, to starting tight end. The Discovery Drills revealed that he was the most consistent player on the team at receiving passes.

The role and position changes, made during the first three days of practice, because of the Discovery Drills, gave the team a whole different look. Coach B said he was able to place players where they fit best, in relation to the other players on the team. Some of the dads, who came to watch practice, were amazed that kids playing in the different positions, with their different roles, had so changed the dynamics of the team.

They said, the team looked "snappy," fast quick, and enthusiastic. The dads were excited to see them play. The Hawks opener was against the team, that finished third the previous year.

Coach B was proud to say that the Hawks ended up, undefeated for the next two years. By the end of his final two years on the team, Huey alone had accumulated 23 touchdowns. According to Coach B, there were too many, personal and team records, that players set and broke, to even talk about without notes.

Coach B said, he was certain that the youth league coaching experience was probably what "relit the coaching fire" within him. Thinking back about those experiences validated for Coach B, many of the lessons that Gramps had taught him.

Coach B said that moving to Louisiana and rebooting his coaching career, after leaving the Coast Guard, may have been, the best thing that ever happened to him as a coach. Louisiana was where he reconnected, with his love of coaching, met Gramps, and discovered his own, "coaching Voice," coaching philosophy, and coaching style. Thinking back on his early coaching days, made him realize even more, that he wished he knew then, what he knows now.

Coach B realized that he had been doing, some of what Gramps taught him, simply by accident. Coach B called it the "plausibility of coaching." Good coaching brings out some of what Gramps talks about, inadvertently. It is just the nature of the profession. But what Gramps is saying, is about purposefulness. Gramps wanted me to do things he talked about on purpose. He wanted me to develop a system, unique to the teams I coach.

No matter the sport, coaches get the most out of their teams, when they smartly place individual players, in the best possible positions, and roles. Positions and roles should be based on direct data, the coaches have collected. The data points, should be in direct comparison with players, on the same team.

The idea, no matter what the sport, is to discover what each player can do best. From the discovered information about each player, the coach could create a certain approach to the sport. The approach taken, should combine the best of each player, then incorporate it into a unique system.

Coaches would be wise to place at least two players in each position. People who are not the starters, must be given appropriate practice time and attention, in the positions, which they will be expected to substitute. As stated earlier, coaches could take the opportunity to place players in the best position for the player, and the team. However, at the same time, each player should have a role specific, to that position assignment.

In relation to basketball, each position should have a role that pertains to every Trigger. In every basketball game, 13 triggers occur intermittingly throughout the contest. Some of the Triggers occur multiple times in each game. There should be a role, for each position, for every Trigger, in all games.

Players, at the very least, should know their specific position and role in response to every trigger. However, for a team to move from really good, to really great, all the players, starters and subs, should know the Trigger responsibilities for every position and every role.

"Ok, I have been listening. What the heck are these Triggers, that you are talking about?"

"Actually, just simple stuff."

"You said that there are 13 of them though. Won't that be hard for players to remember?"

"No. Not really. It's like Gramps use to say all of the time, "There is a time and place, for everything. Always take care of your business first. Camp drills in the off season, systems drills, in season." I try to give the players lots and lots of repetition on, system stuff, in season."

"So, what's the difference, between camp drills, and system drills?"

"System drills should be all about refining the responses to Triggers. Camp drills are to enhance skills. For instance, dribbling drills around cones, two players passing a ball, back and forth, while standing still or running, random shooting, repeatedly moving the ball around the waist, and such are camp drills."

"So are you saying these "camp drills," as you call them, should not be done in season."

"Well, I would never, say never, but I would say rarely, if at all. The team does not really have time for that. Especially if they are aspiring to becoming great, at their system."

"How can spectators figure out what a team's system is?"

"Now that could be a problem, especially when coaches and teams do not actually have a system. Some teams just play offense and defense, and do things that are peculiar to the game of basketball, but do not define a specific system or identity."

"Are you saying that a team cannot win without defining a system?"

"Nope! Not saying that, but I am saying that teams that have actual systems win more consistently, and they know why they won. But more importantly, when a team with a system loses, it is easier to determine why they lost, and have a way to fix it."

"I have heard the term, "Game Plan" used a lot. Is there a difference between game plan and system?"

"Yep! Think of it this way. You heard of David and Goliath, right?"

"Of course, everyone knows about David and Goliath."

"Well, David had so much confidence that he only brought one rock and one sling shot, to the fight."

Coach B and I both broke out laughing after that remark.

Coach B continued, "A coach and the team might have many strategies or game plans, depending on the opponent; but only one system."

"Ok, but what are Triggers?"

"I usually start with giving the players a "Trigger Chart. Take a look."

Coach B reached to grab his backpack, that he had leaned against the table leg. He unzipped the pack and pulled out a blue folder. Inside the folder were several pages of loose paper. Coach B handed me a page. It was, heavy grade, computer copy paper.

Ed Harris

Basketball Triggers

Positions	We make a Shot - Press to trap (1)	We miss shot - lose rebound - Scrabble Defense (2)	We get defense rebound - Outlet Break (3)	We have take-in under our basket (4)	Opponents' cross midcourt on offense - Scramble Trap (5)	Opponents' take-in under own basket - Zone Defense (6)	Opponents' Press-Breaker (7)	We Shoot Free throws	Opponent shoots free throws	Opponents have side take-in on own offense side	We have side take-in on O side	We have side take-in on O side - Stack	We have take-in on D side - man or zone O
1. Point Guard													
2. Shooting Guard													
3. Shooting Forward													
4. Power Forward													
5. Center													

52

After looking at the page, I asked Coach B, "What does this stuff mean?"

"It is a chart graph, of the 13 triggers and 5 positions. It lists all of the major things that occur in a basketball game (The Triggers)."

"Yeah, I can see that, but there are lots of empty boxes. What does that mean?"

Coach B gave a brief explanation, "Each team should have their own unique responses, in each of the spaces for each position. This indicates their own system. How a team responds to each Trigger, defines the team's system."

"So, what do the bold numbers on the chart mean?"

"Those are the **Magnificent Seven**. The seven are the most important, most recurring, most significant of all 13 Triggers. They must be practiced with great repetitiveness during every day of practice."

"Ok, then what do the small numbers in the left column mean?"

"Those are the positions, 1 through 5. Each of those positions have a specific responsibility for each Trigger."

"So, if the 7 Magnificent Triggers, are to be practiced every day, what about the remaining, 6 Covert Triggers?"

"The "Covert 6" must be practiced at least once a week. The Covert or C6 are the Triggers that could change momentum for a team or ultimately win the game for a team. The C6 are kind of like special teams in football. If someone did the research, they would probably discover that the team that executes on special teams best, wins more games."

When I looked at the chart, Coach B had given me, it all started to fit together nicely. I realized when I played, in high school and Junior College, the spot I played would have been, the shooting forward, according to Coach B's vocabulary and methodology. I was starting to see more clearly; about what Coach B was telling me.

Suddenly, it was like an epiphany. I thought, of course, the team that consistently pressures the opponent's side take-ins, controls rebounds after the opponent shoots free throws, makes a high percentage of their own free throws, protects the ball on their own side take - ins, most often wins the game. I remembered when I played ball, those little things, really do add up.

CHAPTER 5

The Magnificent 7

When I was on my way to the office, my sister called, and asked me to take my 10th grade niece, to basketball camp. Seemed as if my sister, had to take my nephew, to a dentist appointment. I really don't know how my sister, keeps up with everything she has going.

My sister, her name is Shannon, is awesome, an outstanding person. I greatly admire and love her. She manages to keep it together, even while being a mom, to a teenager, a fifth grader, and a toddler. It boggles my mind. But I can see, where Zoie gets her tenacity, on the basketball court.

As I was driving, I was thinking fondly about, Coach B's independence from group think. I enjoyed his compelling stories. I found myself thinking about them, even when I was not talking to, or writing about Coach B. I enjoyed listening, just for the fun of the stories. But there was always, some, deeper message as well. I was looking forward to what his message would be today.

When I arrived at the gym, where my niece Zoie, was attending camp, I could not help but notice. Looking at the lettering on their shirts and jerseys, was the clue. There seemed to be teams, from towns up and down, the Missouri side of the Mississippi River.

I had planned to just drop Zoie off, go do some grocery shopping, then return later, to pick her up. Just when I had my plan, solid in my brain, Zoie asked if I would stay and watch her first game.

I asked, "These games aren't official, are they?

"No, not counted as league play, if that's what you mean."

"So, you girls just play games.?

"No, we do drills too."

"How many games do you play, a day?"

"Usually, three in the morning, and three in the afternoon. Five or Six games a day. We play an entire season, worth of games, within a week's time."

"Wow. I did not realize what you were doing here."

"Why don't you stay, and watch a couple of games, Uncle Caleb?"

"Ok, maybe one game. I have some grocery shopping to get done."

I parked the car and walked into the gym with Zoie. Zoie looked at the brackets that were posted on the wall. After a moment of searching, Zoie discovered, on which court, her team would play. I asked Zoie the name of her team. She said, Rockets.

Zoie darted off to find court 15. I looked at the brackets to see how the Rockets were doing so far. The teams were beginning their third day of play. After 12 games the Rockets were 6-6. I instantly started thinking of Coach B. I wondered if the coach of

Zoie's team, was using any of the strategies, Coach B was talking about.

Suddenly I started thinking that watching some of these games could help me understand, more clearly, what Coach B had been talking about. I looked at the chart to list the teams that I would watch throughout the day. I saw that Zoie's team was scheduled to play the Bombers, later in the day. The Bomber's record was 10 - 2, I thought it would be good to see, if I could identify the differences between the two teams. Was it strictly the talent, or was there something else going on. I was excited to start watching.

I texted Coach B, to tell him what I was planning to do, and he got excited. Coach B texted back, asking for the address, and messaging, that he would be right over. I asked him to bring two lawn chairs so we could have a way to sit along the walls to watch the games. I was looking forward to watching the games with Coach B. I wanted to hear, what he had to say about teams, "in real time," while they were actually playing games.

Coach B arrived midway through the first game. I saw him come in through the doors on the far end of the gym, near where the tickets were being sold. I motioned for him, to come over to where I was standing. He had to walk past five games to get to me.

Coach B was stopping at almost every game to watch for a moment. He seemed to find the games to be so interesting, as he moved down the aisle. The exciting part, was that there were ten other games, being played in the other two rooms. This was a basketball fans dream.

As soon as Coach B and I unfolded the chairs, and sat, Coach B opened his backpack. He took out two clipboards, some paper, and handouts he brought along. Coach B handed me one of each, of the things he brought, and he also handed me a pen.

As soon as Coach B's hands were free, we gave the Corona Virus elbow bump, a cordial greeting. Coach B, started talking about the games, almost immediately. He was impressed with the level of talent on the different teams.

Coach B wanted me to look at his handout.

"I made this page so that we could chart the Magnificent 7."

"Why do you want to do that?"

"I want you to see, how frequently the Triggers occur, and how often players on teams, do not have some specific function to perform, during a Trigger event."

When players do not have a specific role, during a Trigger event, it is an indicator, that the team has no system, a minimal system, or an inadequate system. Coaches that teach his or her players a system, have a better chance to win games, and develop players that are good, strong leaders.

Positions	Opponents' press	Control Team makes a shot	Control Team misses shot - loses rebound	Control Team gets defense rebound	Control Team has take-in under Control Team basket	Opponents' cross midcourt on offense	Opponents' take-in under own basket
1. Point Guard							
2. Shooting Guard							
3. Shooting Forward							
4. Strong Forward							
5. Center							

It became very clear, after about five minutes of play, that between us, many tally marks had already accumulated, especially on Coach B's chart. I did not have as many tallies as Coach B, I realized because, I was not as fast as him, at recognizing an actual Trigger, or the correct Trigger, I missed some tallies. Further, Triggers were happening so quick, that I just did not recognize or identify all of them.

Not long after the game was underway, Coach B asked, "Who is that number 30?"

"That's my niece Zoie. She has worn number 30, for Stephen Curry, since she started playing serious basketball. She loves Stephen Curry. She even wants to attend Davidson College, in North Carolina, just like he did."

"Really? What year is she?"

"Sophomore. Well, she will be in 10th grade when school starts. Do you think she's any good?"

"Are you kidding me? That girl can play! Why is she playing in the 3 position?"

"I don't know. Is playing 3, not good? I have not paid much attention to her basketball life. I guess I'm a bad uncle."

"Well, I don't know about that, but if the coach changes her to the point guard and works with her a little, she might be dynamite."

Coach B decided that maybe we should just follow Zoie's games all day. He decided we could see her, and check out the teams, on her schedule for the day. I started to think that Coach B was "pretend," scouting her.

Coach B and I followed Zoie's team, game after game. Coach B asked me at least 100 questions, about the school where Zoie attended, during the school year, her team, her coach, and the other players. We tracked their play, on the Trigger chart for every game.

At the end of the day, we met at "Happy China." Happy China is a restaurant, that serves Asian food, in West County, not far from the Plaza, to have dinner, and review the charts. I guess Coach B was starting to feel sorry for me, and my naivete about the city. So, he selected Happy China in my neighborhood to have dinner.

As soon as we completed filling our plates, to the brim, with enough food for an army to eat, Coach B started analyzing.

> "Do you realize there was not one game, and not one of the 7 Targets where all of the players on Zoie's team, seemed to have specific assignments?"

> "Really? No, I did not notice that."

> "The team did not seem to have a specific plan for the press. It was mostly, whoever got the ball tried to dribble past the press. Every team they played, scored several times on take-ins under the basket. Zoie's team tried to run outlet in the red Zone. It was really hard to watch."

> "Uh, what is the red zone?"

> "Red zone is the area right down the middle of the floor. Worst place to feed an outlet pass. They gave up the ball, what seemed like every other time they threw that pass. The only consistent outlet they had, was when they threw to the baseline. They never once achieved a clean break. If something does not change, and change soon, I don't see

how Zoie is ever going to get a look from Davidson, or any other D1 school."

"Then why don't you coach them?"

"What are you talking about. They already have a coach."

"Actually, they will not have a coach by the time the official season starts. Zoie told me, on my way to drop her at home, the coach told all of the girls that his wife's company, was transferring her to Kansas City. The coach, also announced that he, was going to coach Zoie's, last summer league game, on Saturday and the coach, and his wife were leaving on Sunday."

Coach B was smiling as he thought of the possibilities, "I'm sure that the administration at the school, would say that I am too old."

"I think I could get you in if you want it."

"Let me think about it."

"Well, today is Tuesday. We have a few days."

I could sense that Coach B was really considering the opportunity. He had been away from coaching for 10 years. I think the interview and all of the memories about times with Gramps, were pulling him back to coaching.

In the early morning, the next day, way too early, Coach B called. I sleepily picked up my cell, from the end table, near the bed.

"Caleb Armstrong here."

"This is Coach B. Do you think we could get a chance to see the team practice before the Coach leaves?"

"Uh, I don't know, hmmm, wait a minute, I believe Zoie said her coach was so mad, at the team because they lost 5 and won only three, of the games they played yesterday. He called an early morning practice before their first game today. They were to practice at 7:00."

"Well, where? Where are they practicing? It's six now, so we have an hour."

"At the high school where she attends. MICDS (Mary Institute Country Day Schools)."

"Ok, I know, right where that is. I'll meet you there at 7."

When we met at the school gym, we took a seat, to watch practice. The coach came over to say hello. Actually, we had met before, when Zoie signed up for basketball in her freshman year. He was very friendly and invited us to stay to watch practice.

Coach B busily took notes while he watched, all that occurred during practice.

"Do you think this team could be competitive Coach?"

"Absolutely, there are at least three solidly good players. Your niece, Zoie, #33, and #10.

"Yeah, I think #33's name is Molly, and #10's name is Darcy. Both of those girls are going to be Juniors when school starts."

"I know you think my niece Zoie, Molly and Darcy are good, but what about the one they call Bo? She seems really tough to me."

Coach B looked at the notes he was writing, "Which one is she? What's her number?"

"She's the tallest one, with the dark hair, and the one, long, thick, braid. #44."

"Yeah, after watching for about 30 minutes, if you add number 30 to the four, we mentioned, that would be a very strong starting five."

"Who the heck is #25?"

Coach B pointed across the floor, as he spoke. "She is the slender one over in the corner, along the baseline. You may not be able to see her number from this angle."

"Oh yeah, I see her now, that's Susie, she rarely gets to play."

"What! You have got to be kidding me."

"Coach, really? You have got to be kidding me right now. Of the five you named Almost none of them played much, last season, except for Bo and Zoie."

"How many seniors did they lose, from the team, to graduation?"

"Three I think."

"Were those three seniors, starters?"

"Yep, rain, shine, hail, or blizzard. He would start and play those seniors, for most of the game. I think Molly played mostly because her shooting skill is obvious. Bo played because she is the biggest, toughest player on the team."

Coach B was quiet again, writing incessantly, recording information about the team. I heard Coach B say something, "Too many camp drills. Not specific connections, for the players." I realized that he was talking more to himself than to me.

"What do you mean camp drills?"

"Drills that are not specifically connected to the systems of the team."

"Camp drills are the kind that are used in basketball camps. The coaches that run basketball camps, usually try to keep the drills generic, specific to the game of basketball, but not related to any particular system."

"Why do the coaches at basketball camp do that?"

"Mainly, out of courtesy to the programs, from which the players, that are attending camp originate. Camp coaches do not want to alienate coaches, from the schools, from where the players come."

"What do you mean by, "Not specific connections to the system?"

"Camp drills are used by coaches, at the home school, that have no specific connection to the team program. Camp drills continue to be used, because they are peculiar to the game of basketball, and many coaches have not developed a system for their team."

"So, are you saying that coaches, cannot win if they don't have a system?"

"Winning against competitive teams, without having a system, is highly uncommon. It probably can be done, but it is extremely difficult and not sustainable. Take a look at all the, "Big Dogs," such as UCONN, Notre Dame, Stanford, and many others, now they have systems, my friend."

"Well, what can new coaches or young coaches, do to make sure they have a system, that will sustain victory and build leaders?"

"They could create their systems based on Triggers. Then do drills that are tightly coupled to each of the 13 triggers. The drills should be designed to connect to at least one of the Triggers, especially one of the first seven, the Magnificent 7. Further, all practices should revolve around the Triggers."

Coach B, handed me a page of paper. It was filled with a system for practices, that would be totally related to Triggers. Looked more like Hieroglyphics to me.

Triggers	Time Min	Practice	1 Point Guard	2 Shooting Guard	3 Shooting Forward	4 Power Forward	5 Center
1. Opponents' press	7	Team					
	5	Ind-Skills					
Control Team Shoots Free throws	3	Covert 1					
2. Control Team makes a Shot	7	Team					
	5	Ind-skills					
Opponents have side take-in on own O side	3	Covert 2					
3. Control Team misses a shot and loses rebound	7	Team					
	5	Ind-Skills					
Opponents have side take-in on own D side	3	Covert 3					
4. Control Team gets defense rebound	7	Team					
	5	Ind-Skills					
Opponent shoots free throws	3	Covert 4					
5. Control Team takes-in under our basket	7	Team					
	5	Ind-Skills					
Control Team have side take-in on own O side	3	Covert 5					
6. Opponents' cross midcourt on offense	7	Team					
	5	Ind-Skills					
Control Team has side take-in on own D side	3	Covert 6					
7. Opponents' take-in under own basket	7	Team					
	5	Ind-Skills					
	3	Covert 1					

"Coach, what does all this stuff mean?"

"Just hold on to it. I will explain when we head out to breakfast, after this practice is over."

"What? do you just carry pages of basketball practice plans around with you all of the time? I have to tell you, that is weird Coach."

Coach B smiled as he said, "No, I do not carry it all the time. But when you see me with my backpack, I usually have lots of coaching items in there, along with other important stuff."

"Oh, I see. Interesting," I said with a smile.

"Just hang on. I will explain it all to you at breakfast. It is really very simple. A lot more efficient and effective than what happens at most practices across the country."

Coach B went busily back to taking more notes. The practice was interesting to watch. But Coach B was the real entertainment. One minute he was feverously writing, the next he was saying something, really funny under his breathe, about this drill or that drill. He was really getting into it.

The team was scheduled to have their next game at camp, at 10:30 so the coach cut the practice short. Right after the team huddled to break practice, I waved to Zoie as Coach B and I rushed out to get a quick breakfast, at Sportsman's Park Restaurant. I waved to my sister, she was waiting in the parking lot, to give Zoie a ride to the games.

I was anxious for Coach B to explain the practice chart he had given me. After we got there, took our seats, checked out the menu, and gave the server our orders, I was ready.

"Ok Coach, tell me about this page you gave me." I pulled the page, from my folder, that Coach B had given me.

"What do you call this?"

"The Trigger Practice Chart."

"Oh. Looks complex."

"Not really. You already know the two kinds of triggers. Remember, we talked about that?"

Coach B just started talking, he really got into it as he spoke. He was very animated as he explained the chart.

"Although there are 13 Triggers, remember, there are two kinds. The most important of the Triggers are, what I call the Magnificent 7. The second group are what I call the Covert 6. As you probably noticed, all seven of the M7, are practiced each day. However, each one of the C6 are practiced once a week except C1. C1 is practiced twice a week."

"Coach B, where does it show that on the chart?"

"Easy. Look at the first two columns. You will see the Triggers column, and the second column is the Time & Minutes column. The Triggers column, has when the M7 and C6 should be practiced, during each 15 minute interval during practice."

"Yeah, ok I see that. What does individual, on the chart mean?"

"That, as you see, is in every practice frame. First, the coach starts with a Trigger, that is practiced using five players, most likely to play together in a game. All of the players should be Rotated through, on teams of five practicing the Trigger for about seven minutes. After the seven minutes, individual drills that reinforce the specific Trigger practiced, in the previous seven minutes, should be practiced for five minutes. And, if you look closely, you will see that another three minutes, segment of time, is allotted. During the final three minutes of each 15 minute interval, players, in groups of five, players would practice C6 Triggers."

"Would this occur every day?"

"Yes, each interval should last about 15 minutes. Seven intervals, times fifteen minutes each, would take about 105 minutes. Whether coaches decide to practice for 115 minutes, or 125 minutes, there would be plenty of time, 10 to 20 minutes remaining, after the original 105 minutes. Coaches could use that time, to scrimmage or do additional work and drills on Triggers with players who may be having difficulty."

"Seems like that would be a fairly crisp practice."

"Yes. Not much time for camp drills. Of course, if camp drills, are really important to a coach, he or she could use part of the 10-20 minutes, at the end or beginning of practice for that.

Coaches need to also, not forget, that pre-game warmups, need to be practiced, and special game time situation drills, need to be practiced as well. The extra 10 to 20 minutes, could be used for those things as well. The 10 to 20 minutes do not have to be used for the same thing for every practice."

"So, exactly what kinds of drills need to be done in each interval."

"Great question, Mr. Reporter/Author. For instance, let's just take one that I do. Because each coach can devise their own drills. The main thing, is for whatever drill the coach decides to do, at an interval point, must be tightly coupled to the specific M7 Trigger, that the interval centers on.

Players must understand exactly how the drills connect to the Trigger. For the first Trigger, which is to **have a press breaker,** for the very first game of the season. We would need a full court and half court press breaker.

We would practice cuts, pass routes, and timing in the seven minute team portion. During the individual time segment, we might do inbound passes, with position 4 players and position 1 and 2 players. We might practice long passes from position 1 to position 2 players. Also, long passes from positions 4 and 5 players to the "Jet" (Position 2 players).

We might practice cutoff passes, between position 1 and position 2 players, trying to get the ball to position 3 players. We might practice any detail, of what is expected, on a full or half court press breaker. Depends on the coach, and what he thinks the players need, for that specific Trigger."

"Wow coach, this stuff is precise."

"Yes, when I have a team, I know we are expected to beat the teams that we should win against. But we should also practice, in an effort to prepare, to beat the teams, no one expects us to beat. In order to do that, we have to be crisp, and precise. Using these tactics, we could, beat the teams, we should beat convincingly, and also unexpectedly, beat or lose close, to some of the teams, that people thought, would beat us, by a lot. Now that's what I'm talking about."

"Coach, it is starting to really come out, how competitive you are. Are you sure, you don't want, me to put in a good word at MICDS. You know I am an alumni there."

"I did not, know that. But if I ever get back into coaching,

I kind of have my mind set, on Visitation Academy, where Thad Strobach once coached."

"Alright, but if you change your mind let me know."

CHAPTER 6

System Components

I received a text message from Coach B! I had been trying to get in touch with him for at least a week. I even went by his home, but he was not there. His neighbor had not seen him, and had no idea where he was.

I answered the text, "Where the heck have you been? Where are you?"

Coach B texted back, "I was out of town, but I'm back now. Why don't you meet me at the Hacienda over on Manchester Rd., at 2:00, we can talk then."

I was anxious to hear about where Coach B had been, for over a week. I was excited for 2:00 to come. It had been a while since I visited the Hacienda Restaurant. But, I remembered, they have the best wings. Great place to hang out with friends. I had grown to think of Coach B as a friend. I am no coach, but I have already learned so much, about coaching and about other things, as well, from Coach B.

As usual, when I arrived at the restaurant Coach B was already there. He had grabbed us a table, on the patio, toward the back railing. He had ordered us a carafe of margarita, and some chips and salsa. The server was bringing the wings just as I arrived to take a seat.

Coach B was anxious to begin the conversation, "Caleb Armstrong, my main man! What took you so long?"

"What are you talking about? It is only 1:45, I am here 15 minutes early."

"Well, I am glad you finally got here." Coach B was smiling.

"So, where the heck have you been, for over a week?"

"You remember, I told you about Katy?"

"You mean Gramps' granddaughter?"

Coach B shook his head to indicate yes.

"Yeah, I remember Katy, why?"

"She phoned, told me about Gramps. He had a heart attack."

"I drove over to Columbia, to stay with him while he recovered."

"Columbia? What's he doing in Columbia?"

"Maybe I didn't tell you, but Katy attended Mizzou, on a softball scholarship. Gramps rented an apartment there, so he could be near her, go to practice, see her games, and such. He traveled all over the country to see her games.

After graduation, Katy was hired to teach, and coach at Rock Bridge High School, in Columbia. Gramps remained in Columbia and followed the teams that Katy coached. Katy was the assistant softball coach. Gramps told me she wanted to be a head coach one day. Gramps is dedicated to Katy; he really loves that girl."

"Wow. Now that's what I call a true blue, heavy duty fan. How is he doing?"

"He seems good when I talk to him; but the doctors say, he has about a year or less to live. I intended to stay for a couple of days, but ended up hanging out with him for over a week. For someone who was supposed to die in a few months, Gramps seemed full of life. He insisted that I stay, just to chat about things in general, but also to talk coaching."

"What were the coaching chats about?"

"Gramps had so much to talk about. But the one recurring topic, Gramps was animate about, was my getting back into coaching. He said that a person only has one chance at this life so people ought to do what they love doing. After talking and thinking about it I agreed. Consequently, I am ready to move forward, on getting back into coaching. If you could put in a good word for me, at MICDS or Visitation, I would like either of those two jobs."

"Coach B, it's too late, Man! Sorry my friend, both of those positions have already been filled. I wish you would have said something a few days ago; I might have been able to do something to get you in one of those places."

"Oh no! This is bad news. I promised Gramps I would get going in coaching as soon as possible. I was psyched, to get in the game again."

"Well, why don't you take a look at other jobs. There are several jobs open in the public schools."

"I'm not so sure about the publics, how about charters? Have you heard of openings in charter schools?"

I thought for a moment, then remembered, about the charter that opened a few years ago, in the section of the city called, the Central West End. The school started with only freshmen. The first year, the teams competed on the freshmen level only. With the passing of each year, the teams competed at the successive levels. Next school year, the school's fourth year, the seniors, and some students from the other classes, will compete at the varsity level. The school will have a freshman team, a JV team, and a varsity.

So, I asked Coach B, "What about Cross Roads, In the Central West End?"

"I didn't know they had varsity sports."

"They will, for the first time, next year. They need a coach."

"I don't know about that job. It will probably take years to get that team ready to be competitive."

"Wait a minute, let's look at the data more closely. On the surface, your initial analysis seems to make sense. But when taking a closer look, the previous teams were very successful in past years at each level. The girls' basketball team was 13-7, when they were freshman, during the school's first year. During the second year of the school, the freshmen team was 16-4, and the J.V. team, made up of all sophomores, were 12-8. Last season, the freshmen were 15-5, and the JV comprised of sophomores and juniors were 18-2."

"Wow! The teams have done well. Sounds like they already have a good coach though. They probably don't need me."

"Well, they "had" a good coach, is a more accurate way to put it. Bobby Stallingsworth, was the Head Coach and Athletic Director, at the school since it opened. He recently got offered an assistant women's basketball coaching job at William Jewell College, in Liberty Mo., seems his college roommate, both alumni at Jewell, landed the job, as the Athletic Director there. They needed an assistant in football and basketball, Bobby offered to do basketball and football. He got both jobs. Now, Cross Roads needs a coach."

"What do you think? Would I be a good fit at Cross Roads?"

"Damn right, you would be a tremendous fit. They will love you there."

"Ok, see if you could get me an interview. Let's see what they say."

Once we came to an agreement on the interview prospect, Coach B seemed relieved. He was ready, to talk about his conversation with Gramps. He obviously, was more excited, about getting back into coaching, than he let on. Perhaps a charter school would be just what he needed. The more I thought about it, I was sure that Coach B, would be perfect, for the Cross Roads Crusaders (It is a Christian school).

Coach B and I enjoyed some great tasting, Hacienda Restaurant food. We had conversation about current events, and shared stories about great sport games each of us had seen. I was always alert, for something Coach B would tell me, that I could add to the book, I was writing about him.

As we ate and drank and engaged in fun conversation, I thought about the great career Coach B had. After getting to know him, I was certain his coaching days should not be finished. I was determined to make some calls, later in the day, to see if I could get him an interview with the AD at Cross Roads.

Coach B slowly moved the conversation to his time with Gramps, in the previous week. Coach B seemed really excited, in a low key kind of way, about something concerning coaching, that he and Gramps had discussed. Some breakthrough, for him, he thought, with communication, players to coaches, coaches to players, and between players.

Coach B started talking about his epiphany concerning communication between coach and player, and player to player, before I could even ask a question, or get my recorder and notepad out, and ready to go. I knew, after talking with Coach B, on many occasions, better to let him talk when he's ready. That way, I could get lots, of "good stuff" to write about.

> Coach B said, "While Gramps was talking, I decided to take a small recorder with me, in my backpack, and just turn it on and let it run, while we walked and talked. Katy told me that the doctor had recommended that gramps walk as much as he could every day. So, while I was there, I would get up early, leave the motel, and pick up Gramps, at his apartment. We would go for early morning walks in the park, near his apartment, then stop for breakfast or lunch, depending on the time.
>
> I took the things that Gramps told me, and honed it into my own conception. The whole thing was a sudden, and striking realization for me. Things that Gramps talked to me about have become the foundation of my new system.

I began to realize that, what I will call "Group Think, in Coaching" had me captured. I thought I was being my own person, my own kind of coach. But after many conversations with Gramps, I realized that I had been, just like many of the other coaches. Most of them great people, trying to do the right thing, by the players, but locked in "Group Think," just like me.

Group Think, is when groups, of coaches, buy-in, to a certain framework, idea, or way of thinking, concerning some coaching strategies or concepts. When Coaches, do that, it sometimes becomes a dogmatic mental refrain, to which they all submit. An example, is the idea that man-to-man defense, is a must in basketball.

Group Think ideas, have a "trickle down" effect. Concepts put forward at higher levels of coaching, such as popular D1 colleges, and the NBA, are often adopted by coaches at parallel levels, or lower levels. To some coaches, a Group Think concept or framework of ideas, is like the quest for the "Holy Grail." Coaches within, the Group Think mentality, do not dare go against the concepts. They fear that if they go against Group Think, they will be considered "Bush League" or "Light weight" coaches; not to be legitimately respected, by the group.

In my coaching career, before I knew Gramps, I was heavy into Group Think. I was always worried about what other coaches thought of me, my ideologies, my methods, my system. But now I just keep thinking; if only I knew then, what I know now."

I asked Coach B if there was a brief way he could say, what made the difference in his thinking about coaching; maybe speaking a paragraph or a sentence that sums it all up? I wanted him to give me the gestalt, the big picture, the organized whole; then break it down.

Coach B said, "Things Gramps shared with me are extremely significant. However, my revelations really started when I began to understand, about communication, communication, communication. As silly as it might sound to someone, it probably all started for me, with Renee."

Renee

She had been the star on the middle school team. Renee was about 5'4" and thought of herself as a point guard. When she arrived to play with the high school team, she had a cocky attitude. She and her dad told me, that she should be, the starting point guard on the varsity. We (my assistant and I) were anxious to see her at tryouts.

At tryouts, we discovered that she was not very fast. That was without the ball. However, when she dribbled, she was even slower. After tryouts, we evaluated her as a freshman team player.

We tried her at point guard, on the freshman team. Problem there, was that she was not the best, at decision making either, especially while on the move. We explained, to Renee and her dad, that we were open, to moving her up, to a higher level as she improved. That however, would depend on her performance at the freshman level.

Renee remained on the freshman team all season. Her dad complained, throughout the season, that Renee could display her skills better, if she had been playing with the better players on the varsity. We as a coaching staff did not see, what Renee and her dad, believed about her skills.

The next season, was the second year of the existence of the varsity team. My second year as head coach. And it was Renee's sophomore year of high school. I could not get Renee, and her dad off my mind. I thought perhaps, maybe, I was overlooking something. I began to have second thoughts about where to place Renee.

I decided to revisit the data, and rank the girls in terms of the data points, and categories. I wanted to be fair. Renee was the lead scorer on the freshman team, and had made more three point shots, and free throws than anyone on the team; including varsity players. However, she had more than double the amount of turnovers, as the players on the team, including the varsity.

On the varsity, I knew we needed to score more. So, I swallowed my pride and moved Renee to varsity. She and her dad were ecstatic, the caveat however; her position would be changed to #3, shooting forward. I hoped that by moving her to the #3 position it would help curtail the turnovers.

The idea was to keep the ball in her hands only to shoot. We would organize things so that her propensity, to turn over the ball would be minimized. But at the same time, her shooting opportunities would be maximized.

Renee and her dad had different ideas. They thought that Renee was a great ball handler and passer. Renee and her dad were really strong, "Renee fans." Not a lot of regard for the team as a whole.

Renee was constantly out of place in practice, and in games. She was regularly putting herself in a position to take the outlet pass, or getting the defensive rebound. Once she secured a rebound, Renee immediately tried, to speed dribble down the center of the court. When Renee tried to speed dribble, down the center of the floor, opponents on defense would often steal the ball. She had a tough season.

The second year, our goal was to have 10 or more wins. We had nine wins going into the last game of the season. There were 15 seconds remaining in the game. We were down by two. I called time out. We had a take-in at the opponent's baseline. We had to go full court to get a shot.

We suspected the opponents would press full court. I put Renee back into the game (She was sitting because of turnovers and constantly being out of place). However, we needed her three point shot at that moment. My message to the team was to first run our press breaker. The idea was to get the ball across midcourt, and pass it to Renee, on the three point arc.

I told Renee to shoot the three pointer, if she was open. But if not, pass the ball back to Hope, the point guard. Hope would then shoot the three pointer. We broke the huddle to end the time out.

The strong forward, made a clean toss-in to Hope, the point guard. Everyone was headed to the appropriate spots. As we expected, the defense jumped into their press. Not a surprise, we had talked about that during the time out. Our Center, had located in the middle circle. Since the ball came in on the right side, to Hope; the center moved toward the ball side, sideline.

However, Renee for some reason, was trying to get the inbound pass thrown to her, on the left side of the floor. Renee was supposed to run to the ball side corner to be ready to take the three point shot. Instead, Renee had completely cut off, our other guard. Our number two player, Stephie, went immediately toward the middle, but seeing that Renee, had taken the middle, Stephie (Not a strong shooter) went to our baseline, weakside, corner.

When Hope received the inbound pass, the defense shifted. Their middle defender followed Molly, our center, to the outside. Molly received the pass from our point guard. The middle of the floor was empty; that is except for Renee. Renee was right where our point guard, would have been cutting. Instead, Molly threw the ball to the right place, but to the wrong person, Renee.

Renee caught the ball just across the midcourt line. She took one dribble, a huge elongated step, and flung the ball at the goal. The shot missed the whole goal. One of their players got hold of the ball, then started to dribble up court. Their coach called out a code for them, and they just held the ball, for five seconds and the game was over.

When Coach B stopped, at the end of that story about Renee, I felt angry with Renee and I wasn't even there.

I said, "How did the team react? How did the fans react? What did Renee and her dad have to say?

"We were all upset as you might imagine. Most everyone on the team was angry at Renee. Most of the fans were just upset that we lost. I talked to the team after the game briefly, then let them go say hello to their parents and thank them for coming to support us.

Renee and her dad approached me after the team release. They said that we should have inbounded the ball to Renee, and cleared out, so that Renee, could dribble up to the three point line, and take a comfortable shot. I just listened, put away the balls then went home."

As we continued our conversation, Coach B, in referring to the Renee story, as it compared to his conversation with Gramps, just shook his head.

Coach B softly said, "Communication, communication, communication. If only I knew then, what I know now."

"Are you saying, that Renee's mistakes were somehow your fault?"

"Yep! All my fault.

"I don't get it. How was that your fault?"

"Communication! I did not communicate well enough, thorough enough, clearly enough, what they were to do."

"Well how did Renee do her junior year?"

"Don't know, Mom and Dad got a divorce. Renee went to live with her maternal grandmother, somewhere in Oregon. Never heard anything else about her. I count her as one I lost. Not a good moment for me."

I still didn't get it. I could not see how what happened, with Renee, could have possibly been Coach B's fault. I decided to move the conversation forward. I thought maybe I would understand later.

Coach B started talking about his realizations, that were stirred by his conversation with Gramps. He said it was all to do with developing a system. Coach B explained that he realized that he, never really had a solid system, for his teams. Actually, he just had a collection of fundamentals and skills that the players implemented to play games. Coach B said that the teams he played against were mostly just like his.

Most of the teams along with his, according to Coach B, probably spent most of their practice time, doing a collection of camp drills, meshed together around a bunch of, unrelated to games, running and exercises. Most of the coaches, Coach B said, he played against, when talking about their practices, must have spent more than 60 percent of practice time doing offense plays. They had a number of plays; they would have players run repeatedly. If the opposing coaches, were anything like him, Coach B said, the players probably heard the words, "Stop! Let's do it again" regularly.

According to Coach B, after thinking about his talks with Gramps, finally realized, his practices were being chewed up, with offense plays, and unrelated to games, defense drills. Since his teams were winning, in a "hit or miss" fashion, Coach B said, he didn't really realize what was actually happening. He had been, according to him, in some kind of coach's silent state of, self-inflected drone-like behavior. Coach B said, after coming to understand what Gramps had been trying to tell him, that maybe, perhaps, he could cure his own coaching insanity; doing the same drills, and group thinking, over and over again, but expecting different results.

Coach B said that, when he visited Gramps in Columbia, Gramps had finally gotten through to him. Systems are created, and the coaching elixir, that leads to consistent winning, are formulated during practice. Practices should be comprised of the repetition of two components, Essential Keys, and Coaching Oversights.

Coach B said that, if ever he got his hands on a team, as head coach again, he would do things totally different, than he had before, when he was head coach.

I asked him, "Different, how?"

Coach B said, "In almost every way, things would be different."

"Give me a, for instance."

Coach B paused to think for a moment. It looked as if, Coach B was trying to determine where to begin, with his explanation.

"Well, to keep things simple, I would focus on the **Essential Keys and Coaching Oversight.** The **Essential Keys** consist of, teaching the players to recognize and identify the 13 triggers; consisting of the Magnificent 7 and the Covert 6 triggers. It is important that players can identify and be ready to respond to each Trigger."

"Don't most coaches yell things out, to the players, that tell them how to respond, to what is happening on the floor. Are you saying that coaches should not yell out information to their teams?"

"No. What I am saying is that, the players, should be coached to identify the Targets, on their own, then the coach's voice, from the bench, would merely be a helpful reminder."

I was not totally convinced, "I don't see why Essential Keys should be seen as something different. Help me understand why this is important."

"Essential Keys are not just for recognizing and identifying Triggers; but also, for learning, and understanding the responses to the triggers. When coaches introduce the Essential Keys, players learn the codes of the system, and such alerts as, cues and options to look for."

"What you are talking about, would seem to me, to be a no brainer. Don't most coaches do that anyway?"

"Well, kinda sorta. Coaches speak in a language that sometimes, not all of the players, are understanding, in the same way, what they are collectively hearing, for instance, some coaches, often use different words, that mean the same thing. This confuses some of the players, or at least slows their reaction time, because they have to interpret before they respond."

"Ok, give me an example?"

"On the box or the square, sideline or outline, lane or paint, euro-step or step around, arc or circle. But it does not stop there, sometimes coaches use two or more code words, that mean the same thing. For instance, when coaches want players, to retreat, to defend the goal; the coach might say, "get back or fill the lane, or defense, or fire." Even worse, coaches sometimes use the same code that means different things in different situations. This drives players and coaches crazy. Coaches get crazy over this because they cannot understand, why some of the players don't know the codes. Players get crazy, because they do not understand why the coach has one code that means several things. This is coach-inflicted confusion, leading to self-destruction on the floor."

"Yeah, I could see how, that could be a problem."

"Coaches ought to take the time to "flush out" their language from time to time. Coaches sometimes need to make sure they, and their players, are using the same language, the same codes. I remember being at a practice where I was a volunteer coach, and the coach pulled the team together in a circle to tell them, they were going to work on taking the ball in from the side. He asked the team, what they should call the take-in play? One player shouted an idea for a code, another player suggested a color as the code, a third player suggested the name of an object. It was a dilemma. Then one of the players suggested they simply call it, Side Take-in."

I started laughing at the simplicity of the final suggestion, "Now that was genius." I comically thought.

Coach B was smiling too, as he said, "Yeah, right, so the head coach said, they would start off, calling it side-take-in, until they thought of something better. So often coaches, create so much jargon and verbiage, within their program until it is hard for players, or even the coaches themselves to keep track."

"So, what is the solution?"

"I don't know about "The Solution" but my recommendation would be to follow the old coaching adage, "KISS," Keep it simple stupid. I of course, would not call anyone stupid, but I understand the sentiment.

I usually suggest, that coaches might seek to, **simplify**, **clarify**, and **demystify** things for people. When preparing, concerning how a coach will speak something to players, the coach could use a reverse method, or UBD (Understanding by Design - Grant Wiggins). No matter the coaching method; before speaking, a coach should think about how he or she want the players to hear and interpret. Then prepare how he or she will speak."

I asked, "How can players and even coaches, remember all this stuff?"

"Often they don't. That's why coaches should write codes and possible options, that match certain codes, in a glossary. A glossary that coaches should review and edit, at least monthly, during the season, and then do a deep cleansing, at the end of each season. Unnecessary or obsolete terms and codes, could be purged."

"Man! I did not know that all this stuff goes on in coaching."

"Well, that's the point. It should be going on, if a coach wants to have an actual system that drives his or her programs. But, often, none of this actually occurs in most programs. Nevertheless, just as important as the codes are the alerts."

"I have never heard you talk about alerts."

"Alerts are basically built around the scouting report, in preparation for the next opponent. Cues that the opponent, inadvertently reveals, many times, offers options to exploit. Not paying attention to cues and options, is like leaving out the baking soda, when baking a cake. In the end, something that looks like a cake, might be the result; but it probably tastes terrible. In other words, the team may still win, but it will, more often than not, be ugly."

I said aloud, what I was thinking, "This is a lot to remember."

"Yes, coaching is very cerebral. So much is involved, it is difficult to get it all out; when speaking in general terms. For example, there is a lot more to say and explain about the essentials, but the coaching oversights are also important."

"How are Essential Keys and Coaching Oversight different?"

"Essential Keys are things that must be drilled with regularity and consistency during every practice. Coaching Oversight must be planned and strategized sometimes before, sometimes during, and sometimes after games. Essential Keys must be tightly coupled with Coaching Oversights."

"Give me some examples of what you call Coaching Oversight?"

"Ok. Oversight stuff, is like having specific Game Plans, and strategies. The coaches could introduce the game plans at practice, that are designed to defeat a specific opponent. Also, coaches should, define player positions, and roles for every reaction and every option. All Alerts should be fortified by reinforcement of the positions and roles.

There should be a backup for each player's appropriate action. An easy, and understandable example, might be when a coach makes the decision, that players will switch on, off ball screens, but fight over the screen on, on-ball screens."

"Ok. I can visualize that. But, isn't that done in practice."

"Yes, it is repeated, in practice, to gain muscle memory, but it is decided, at some point, before practice. It is the same, with decisions about positions, and roles. When subbing in different positions, players should be expected to use the roles designed for the specific positions. Also, during practice, coaches should use specific team language and codes, when reminding players, while they are moving, about the automatics, the codes, and the rules. This will most often cause quick and easy translations and interpretations during games."

I began to understand that coaching, by system is really complex, but at the same time tight. I was anxious to actually see Coach B in action. I was excited to see Coach B coaching his own team; in practice and in games.

Coach B and I had to end the meeting. We both had other things we had to do. Coach B said he had to pick up his dog from the kennel, and I had some work related stuff to tend to. Coach B and I, set up a meeting, time and place, for the next day. Coach B departed. I paid the bill; sat for a few minutes longer, then headed back to my apartment. I was continuing to work from home. Another byproduct, for me, of Corona Virus.

Later that afternoon, as promised, I gave the Athletic Director, Joe Romano, at the Cross Roads Academy, a call. I told Joe, about Coach B and strongly suggested, Coach B be considered, for the Head Women's Basketball coaching position, at Crossroads Academy. Joe and I had taken some graduate classes together, and I had written a few favorable articles, about Crossroads Academy, over the years, as they were getting started, so I hoped Joe felt a little obligated.

Long story short. Coach B got the job! They already love him there. I phoned Coach B as soon as I heard the news. After a bunch of hoorays, and noise making on the phone I got right to business.

"Coach, how about I follow you through the first season, and add what I learn from watching you coach, to the book?"

"Absolutely!"

"Let me know when you get started. I will be there."

"Will do."

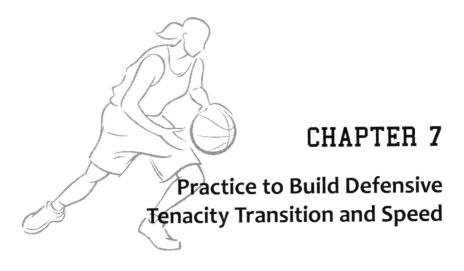

CHAPTER 7

Practice to Build Defensive Tenacity Transition and Speed

I received the text at the "Ungodly time of 2:00 AM. It was Coach B.

"Caleb, Coach B here. You are not going to believe this! I got Katy the job as teacher and coach at Crossroads!"

"What? Gramps' Katy?"

"Yes! She is going to be the Head Softball Coach."

"That is really very cool."

"Oh nooo, there is more my friend, there is more!"

"More? What's more?"

"She is going to be one of my assistant basketball coaches. She is going to coach the JV."

"That is really nice of you to get her a job Coach. This is awesome, an ex-player of yours, as an assistant coach. Should be a great start to the season."

"Get this though, Gramps is going to be my assistant on the Varsity!"

"You have got to be kidding me! No way!"

"Yes way!"

Coach B and I were really excited. Two weeks later I met him at Crossroads for his first practice. Coach B met me at the front door of the gym. He told me he had asked me to come, 30 minutes early. He wanted to explain how practice, during the first day, and the first few weeks, before the first game, would work.

Coach B told me that he would meet with the coaches first, to explain the System's Components. Then he and his assistant coaches, would meet with the players, who were trying out, for the team. Coach B said he wanted me to hear the overview of the system, as he would tell the coaches; and later the players. Coach B thought, this would help me understand, so that as I wrote the book, about Coach B, I would have a more intimate realization, of Coach B's two component system, of Essential Keys and Coaching Oversight.

When the coaches arrived, Coach B introduced me to Tony Rick (A hold over from the previous program), Katy and to Gramps. Not to have met Katy and Gramps was odd, as I thought about it. Coach B and I spent many meetings together where Katy and Gramps were often mentioned within the context of the conversations. However, I had never met either of them.

Coach B explained that I would be shadowing the program, to collect information about the book I was writing. After a few pleasantries and cordiality, Coach B started to explain. He talked about how he wanted the coaches to approach teaching the players throughout the season.

Coach B started by saying, "Thanks everyone for coming and for being a part of this first year varsity program. I am really excited to get started."

Gramps asked, "Have you seen any of the girls play? Do we have any talent?"

Katy said, "I was wondering the same thing. What do we have to work with? How many girls have signed up?"

Coach B responded, "Well coaches, we are going to see, in about 30 minutes. The players will be arriving to participate in a battery of events, that will reveal their talent, or lack of talent. Either way, we will find a way, to make them into the best team they can be."

Coach B held up two pages of paper. He said that he wanted to talk through the pages with us, before the first practice. He explained that we would probably have questions. He wanted us to take the pages home, after practice, to look them over.

Girls Basketball Discovery Event Tally Sheet
Scoring (10-7-4 Points per activity — Games - play to
10 by 2 winner gets 10 points loser 7)

Players	Basketball Skills	Basketball Skills	Basketball Skills	Basketball Skills	Total
	Backward Run _____ Karaoke races _____ 1 V 1 _____	Forward races _____ Dribble Race _____ 3 v 3 _____	Lay-ups _____ Free throws _____ 4 v 4 _____	3-point shots _____ Mikan Drill _____	
	Backward Run _____ Karaoke races _____ 1 V 1 _____	Forward races _____ Dribble Race _____ 3 v 3 _____	Lay-ups _____ Free throws _____ 4 v 4 _____	3-point shots _____ Mikan Drill _____	
	Backward Run _____ Karaoke races _____ 1 V 1 _____	Forward races _____ Dribble Race _____ 3 v 3 _____	Lay-ups _____ Free throws _____ 4 v 4 _____	3-point shots _____ Mikan Drill _____	
	Backward Run _____ Karaoke races _____ 1 V 1 _____	Forward races _____ Dribble Race _____ 3 v 3 _____	Lay-ups _____ Free throws _____ 4 v 4 _____	3-point shots _____ Mikan Drill _____	
	Backward Run _____ Karaoke races _____ 1 V 1 _____	Forward races _____ Dribble Race _____ 3 v 3 _____	Lay-ups _____ Free throws _____ 4 v 4 _____	3-point shots _____ Mikan Drill _____	
	Backward Run _____ Karaoke races _____ 1 V 1 _____	Forward races _____ Dribble Race _____ 3 v 3 _____	Lay-ups _____ Free throws _____ 4 v 4 _____	3-point shots _____ Mikan Drill _____	
	Backward Run _____ Karaoke races _____ 1 V 1 _____	Forward races _____ Dribble Race _____ 3 v 3 _____	Lay-ups _____ Free throws _____ 4 v 4 _____	3-point shots _____ Mikan Drill _____	
	Backward Run _____ Karaoke races _____ 1 V 1 _____	Forward races _____ Dribble Race _____ 3 v 3 _____	Lay-ups _____ Free throws _____ 4 v 4 _____	3-point shots _____ Mikan Drill _____	
	Backward Run _____ Karaoke races _____ 1 V 1 _____	Forward races _____ Dribble Race _____ 3 v 3 _____	Lay-ups _____ Free throws _____ 4 v 4 _____	3-point shots _____ Mikan Drill _____	
	Backward Run _____ Karaoke races _____ 1 V 1 _____	Forward races _____ Dribble Race _____ 3 v 3 _____	Lay-ups _____ Free throws _____ 4 v 4 _____	3-point shots _____ Mikan Drill _____	
	Backward Run _____ Karaoke races _____ 1 V 1 _____	Forward races _____ Dribble Race _____ 3 v 3 _____	Lay-ups _____ Free throws _____ 4 v 4 _____	3-point shots _____ Mikan Drill _____	
	Backward Run _____ Karaoke races _____ 1 V 1 _____	Forward races _____ Dribble Race _____ 3 v 3 _____	Lay-ups _____ Free throws _____ 4 v 4 _____	3-point shots _____ Mikan Drill _____	
	Backward Run _____ Karaoke races _____ 1 V 1 _____	Forward races _____ Dribble Race _____ 3 v 3 _____	Lay-ups _____ Free throws _____ 4 v 4 _____	3-point shots _____ Mikan Drill _____	
	Backward Run _____ Karaoke races _____ 1 V 1 _____	Forward races _____ Dribble Race _____ 3 v 3 _____	Lay-ups _____ Free throws _____ 4 v 4 _____	3-point shots _____ Mikan Drill _____	
	Backward Run _____ Karaoke races _____ 1 V 1 _____	Forward races _____ Dribble Race _____ 3 v 3 _____	Lay-ups _____ Free throws _____ 4 v 4 _____	3-point shots _____ Mikan Drill _____	
	Backward Run _____ Karaoke races _____ 1 V 1 _____	Forward races _____ Dribble Race _____ 3 v 3 _____	Lay-ups _____ Free throws _____ 4 v 4 _____	3-point shots _____ Mikan Drill _____	

Coach B said that we would meet again, tomorrow before practice, to answer the initial questions one or more of us had.

Coach B explained that Discovery Events, would be used to test the skills of each player, as she compares to the other players on the team. Coach B further explained that although the first two days of practice would be dedicated, to player participation in the Discovery Events, the coaches would be evaluating for possible position placement. Coach B asked that we take a look at the listed Discovery Events to see what else coaches would be looking for during practice.

Discovery Events

All of us looked at the sheet as Coach B explained. On the Discovery Event page, was a tally sheet with the scoring rubric. Players would be ranked in comparison to each other. For instance, players finishing in first place, in each event, would receive ten points. Second place finishers, would receive seven points, and third place finishers, would receive 4 points. The 1 on 1, 3 on 3, and 4 on 4 games, would be played to ten points scores. The winning team would receive 10 points, the other team would receive 7 points.

Each player would compete against every player in their position pool. Players would be placed on 3 on 3 and 4 on 4 teams according to position pool and age. Players would be placed on teams where the size and age of the players are matched as close as possible. Each team would have a rebounder, forward, and guard (As the players have self-selected).

Coach B told us about the individual player events. The events were divided into two parts, agility and running races, and shooting competition. Players, race doing agility and run events.

Players race against every person in their position pool two times. As they sign-in to practice, each player would self-identify, to one of four positions, point guard, wing, forward, or center. The categories for ball handling agility races and shooting competition are, Items one through eight:

1. Ball handling races
    *   Item 1-Karaoke agility races
    *   Item 2-Forward run
    *   Item 3-Backward Run
    *   Item 4-Dribbling Race

2. Shooting competition
    *   Item 5-Mikan
    *   Item 6-Layups
    *   Item 7-Free throws
    *   Item 8-5-points shots

The winners, in each agility race, would receive ten points. second place finishers would receive seven points. Those finishing third would receive four points. For shooting drills, each player would get ten shots in each shooting category, item 5, 6, 7, and 8; competing against the players in the same pool.

The winners, in each category items, 5, 6, 7, and 8, would receive ten points. Those finishing with the second most shots made of the ten, in each category items, 5, 6, 7, and 8, as compared to others in their pool, would receive seven points. Those finishing with the third most shots made, of the ten, in each category items, 5, 6, 7, and 8, as compared to others in their pool, would receive four points.

The points awarded for other shots, would also hold true, for the 5 - spot - shot category. 10 shots would be taken from each of the 5 spots. The spots would be:

- baseline 3 pointers, from left and right side,
- wing shots from left and right side (2 point shots)
- 3 point shots from the top of the key.

The number of shots made, of the 50 shots taken, by each player, would be summed. The player with the most shots made of the 10 taken for each item, would receive ten points, the player with the second amount of shots made would receive seven points, the player with the third amount of shots made of the 50, would be awarded four points.

Each player's points would be summed. The players would be ranked four ways. One ranking would be by pool, another ranking would be by category, a third ranking would be by item, and a fourth ranking would be overall score.

Initially, using the data from the Discovery Events, players would be placed on three teams at each level, varsity, Junior varsity, and freshman teams. Team one at the varsity level could consist of the top scoring players from each pool, the top scoring player from each category, the top scoring player from each item, and the player with the highest number of points overall. Varsity, team two, could consist of players with the second highest score in each category. Varsity, team three could consist of the five players who scored the third highest points in each category.

Three teams would be formed at the junior varsity level, by placing the remaining players, on three teams, also based on data from the Discovery Events. The process at the junior varsity level would mirror the process at the varsity level. Once the three teams at the varsity level and the three teams at the junior varsity level is completed. The same process should be used at the freshman level to initially placing players in appropriate levels. Coaches should keep in mind that seniors should not be placed on junior varsity, or freshman level teams. Seniors are varsity only.

Katy was excited to have an objective rubric, by which to evaluate the players. She was happy to have a player evaluation document, based on merit; to show to players, and to show to parents. A document that displays, why players were initially placed, where they were placed, would exude fairness, and transparency. Katy told us about an experience that she had coaching softball that related to activating the Discovery Events. Katy told us:

Mr. Hambright

When I was coaching softball in the summer leagues, I pulled a very good freshman shortstop named Abby Hambright, up to varsity to be a backup outfielder. I already had several good upperclassmen infielders. Abby was probably the tenth best hitter on the team, and she was new in town, so I thought it might help her fit in, and she might help us.

We had a pretty good team that year. I had two players that had signed D1 letters of intent to attend Alabama and Oklahoma State. We were tied for first place and had been picked in the preseason to win it all. I was very excited for that team.

Everything was going pretty well except for having to deal with Abby's Dad, Mr. Hambright. Gramps taught me that most parents, just want the best for their kids. Parents want their children to be successful. The main thing coaches have to do is, make sure parents understand, that the athletes, and parents, have high aspirations for the team as a whole. But also, each parent has personal aspirations for his or her particular parent child. Coaches have to explain, that parents and coaches, are on the same team, when it comes to a parent's child.

However, sometimes a parent's aspirations for their child clouds their "long view" of the team as a whole. For instance, Mr. Hambright was furious with me because Abby was not the starting shortstop on the team. Mr. Hambright also insisted that Abby should be hitting, in the leadoff position. To support his point of view, Mr. Hambright pointed to the fact, that Abby had been, an all-star player as shortstop, for three years running, on her Amateur Athletic Union (AAU) softball team.

Even after I pointed out that our starting shortstop, Brody Mack, had already graduated from high school, and was absolutely the best player I had ever coached, Mr. Hambright was not deterred. I explained that his daughter was a very strong freshman player, but she was not as big or as strong as Brody right now.

I told Mr. Hambright that Brody had been a four year starter, at shortstop on the varsity and that, B-Mack as the players called her, had already signed, to play at Oklahoma State. Further, she was projected to be a starter there as a freshman. She had a boat load of honors, from playing high school ball. She made first team all-state, two years in a row, and was hitting over 400.

I knew that Mr. Hambright, had just moved to town, and probably did not know the players well yet. I explained that his daughter Abby was the only freshman that had been moved up to varsity. Quite an accomplishment, a big deal in the community. I explained that it was something for which, she and he, could be very proud.

The explanations calmed him a little, but it would have been so great, to have had some data. Data that showed head to head competition points, between players in the same positions, would have been terrific to have. The players and parents could see how each player compared, skill-wise to others, on the team. This would have offered transparency.

Had I known about Discovery Events at the time, I think it would have changed the whole culture and climate, of the team, much for the better.

I realized that Mr. Hambright and I, did not have the good fortune, of having common data, on which to reflect, when we were having the conversations, about Abby's position on the team.

I am so looking forward to having the information that the Discovery Events will provide. It will be so good to see the raw scores. But, the culminations of scores, in categories and among items, will be invaluable as we make coaching decisions for the team.

After listening to the story about Mr. Hambright and his daughter Abby, Coach B asked, "How did things turn out with Abby playing on the team?"

Katy replied, "Actually she did well. She got a chance to do some pinch base running, she pinch hit, a couple of times. She got a walk and hit into a fielder's choice once. Off that play she stole second, and scored on the single, hit by the next player at bat. She did good."

Coach B continued, "How about Mr. Hambright? How did things turn out with him?"

"We never warmed up to each other. He was not happy that Abby never played short-stop all season. Now that I look back, I probably should have played her there, more often."

I was curious, "Did you ever have the opportunity to play her there?"

"Yes, there were several opportunities."

Gramps looked at Katy smiling, then talking to the rest of us but really talking to her as well said, "She remembers that I did suggest to play her. It would have been not only wise, but also, the right thing to do. Coaches should never hold it against a player, or even cause, it to look like the player is being punished, because of miss guided acts by her parents."

We all understood the lesson Gramps told us at that moment. After a few seconds of unintended, but thoughtful silence, Coach B began to tell the coaches and me about the Triggers, and how they would be practiced. Coach B explained about practicing the 13 Triggers every week to prepare for competition. Coach B talked about it in this way:

Triggers and Responses

Coach B said, "I want us to make certain, that a balance is struck, in practice, concerning Triggers. Preparation and balance, during practice, should convince the players they are ready to meet the challenges of a game. Players gain confidence, when they are certain, of position assignments and roles. Knowledge by position, assignments, and roles, in general and specifically, as it pertains to the upcoming opponents, heightens a player's poise."

Coach B explained that each Trigger would have 15 minute practice time splits. Seven minutes in each 15 minute split, will be devoted, to team organization for each Target. Five minutes of each 15 minute split, will focus on drills for individual players, that directly relate to the seven minute split for team organization. Three minutes of each 15 minute split, will be dedicated to one of the Covert 6 Triggers.

All practices, according to Coach B, will last not more than two hours and last an average time span of 90 minutes. After the seven fifteen minute time splits, there will be time remaining within the two hour time limit, to intermittingly do something, outside the 15 minute intervals, that the coach feels is important to cover.

Coach B handed us the other sheet, he had shown us earlier, as he verbally outlined the Targets, for the assistant coaches and me. Coach B told us that the players would get many reps, within the 15 minutes intervals. The idea was that each player would know the Triggers, backward and forward, by the first game. Coach B began the explanation:

Triggers	Time Min	Practice	1 Point Guard	2 Shooting Guard	3 Shooting Forward	4 Power Forward	5 Center
1. Opponents' press	7	Team					
	5	Ind-Skills					
Control Team Shoots Free throws	3	Covert 1					
2. Control Team makes a Shot	7	Team					
	5	Ind-skills					
Opponents have side take-in on own O side	3	Covert 2					
3. Control Team misses a shot and loses rebound	7	Team					
	5	Ind-Skills					
Opponents have side take-in on own D side	3	Covert 3					
4. Control Team gets defense rebound	7	Team					
	5	Ind-Skills					
Opponent shoots free throws	3	Covert 4					
5. Control Team takes-in under our basket	7	Team					
	5	Ind-Skills					
Control Team have side take-in on own O side	3	Covert 5					
6. Opponents' cross midcourt on offense	7	Team					
	5	Ind-Skills					
Control Team has side take-in on own D side	3	Covert 6					
7. Opponents' take-in under own basket	7	Team					
	5	Ind-Skills					
	3	Covert 1					

All coaches can have their ways to systemize their teams. But this is the way we will play.

Target 1:
(Opponents Press either full or half court)
- **Practice Time Splits** -
  (Team 7 minutes, Individual, 5 minutes, Covert, 3minutes)
- **Response to Target 1** -
  (Breaker - Full or half court)
  A. **Main Coaching Points for the team** - Players get to starting spots fast
     - Player 4 in-bound the ball, then move to follow ball down court at controlled pace
     - Player 3 get to the nearest sideline, slide from midcourt to Control Team Foul-line extended to get open for a pass
     - Player 2 get to the opposite side of floor as player 1, slide from opponent's foul-line extended to five second line to get open for a pass
     - Player 1 get to the best, most open toss in spot, turn to face up-court looking for an open pass,
     - Player 5 get to the middle circle, slide back and forth between middle circle and top of key on our team's part of floor
  B. **Main Coaching Points for individuals** - Short crisp passes, minimal dribbling - Only dribble to create a passing lane, or to move the ball toward our team's basket - get the ball to the middle of the press, or down the sideline quickly, look for an easy layup first, then look for outside shot.
- **Covert 1** -
  (Our team shoots free throws)
  A. **Main Coaching Points for the team** - Aggressively block out and hustle for the rebound by creating the rebounding triangle (Player 4 and 5 cover the blocks,

Player 3 covers the bottom of the lane circle); gather rebound then, jump right back up with the shot, try to get fouled

B. **Main Coaching points for individuals** - Same as for the team, but also be ready to press after our Team makes the basket, or be ready to Scramble if the opponents get the rebound

Target 2:
(Opponent, grabs a defensive rebound, or crosses midcourt)

- **Practice Time Splits** -
  (Team 7 minutes, Individual, 5 minutes, Covert, 3minutes)
- **Response to Target 2** -
  (**SCRAMBLE** - Our Team gets back fast, in the paint, to defend our goal - Use either a Trap, 23 Zone, or man defense - this will be pre-determined at team, planning.)
  - A. **Main Coaching Points for the team** - (Get a stop - Retreat back into the paint to regroup into a planned response.)
  - B. **Main Coaching Points for individuals** - (Protect the paint first, get at least one foot, in the lane before you move to planned defensive response. Do not foul - Look to steal passes not dribbles.)
- **Covert 2** -
  (**Opponent shoots free throws**)
  - A. **Main Coaching Points for team** - Aggressively block out and hustle for the rebound, by creating the rebounding triangle; gather rebound then **OUTLET** to fast break transition. Be quick, be fast, but don't be in a hurry.
  - B. **Main Coaching points for individuals** - Same as for the team, but also be ready to run **Breaker,** if the opponent makes the basket, or be ready to Outlet, if our Team gets the rebound.

Target 3:
(Opponent's take-in, under their own basket)

- **Practice Time Splits** -
  (Team 7 minutes, Individual, 5 minutes, Covert, 3minutes)
- **Response** -
  (23 Defense should be activated (This could be different by opponent - This is a decision made in practice, or during down time in the game)
  A. **Main Coaching Points for the team** - (close off passing lanes, invite outside passes, do not foul. Look to steal passes not dribbles. Tie up dribbles by player 4 and 5, look for jump ball call)
  B. **Main Coaching Points for individuals** - Hands straight up to challenge shot, if they get ball in. If our team gets a steal, or rebound look to OUTLET, and fast break transition. Be quick, be fast, but don't be in a hurry.
- **Covert 3** -
  Opponents have side take-in on own offense side
  A. **Main Coaching Points for team** - Run BANDITS against side take-ins - Everyone runs tight man to man defense, Position 5 player guards the in-bounder (A switch can be made later if necessary), All of our players, Deny, Deny, Deny - Looking for a 5 second call. Once in Bandits, stay in Bandits, until our team returns to offense.
  B. **Main Coaching points for individuals** - Same as for the team, play defense by moving feet, keep hands out and away from opponent, do not reach, but also be ready to run, fast break transition, if a steal is made. Be quick, be fast, but don't be in a hurry.

Target 4:
(When our team makes a Shot)
- **Practice Time Splits** -
  (Team 7 minutes, Individual, 5 minutes, Covert, 3minutes)
- **Response** - **Press, Press, Press**
  A. **Main Coaching Points for the team** - Form a 1-2-1-1 formation, methodically rotate on passes, Wings invite passes in front, but discourage passes to an opponent behind, on the strong side of the floor. If ball is in the Red Zone (Middle of the floor) all sides are strong. attack to pinch only on dribbles.
  B. **Main Coaching Points for individuals** - Same as team, do not foul, make the opponents play in front of our team's defense, discourage long passes behind.
     - Wings are always on the ball if the ball is on that side of the floor. The weak-side wing replaces player 4, in the middle once player 4 leaves the middle to pursue an interception or to pinch with the ball-side wing.
     - Once the ball crosses mid-court, the weak-side wing must cover the back-side block.
     - The ball-side wing must chase, and pressure to the ball, looking for help with a pinch, from the point, or the 4 player
     - When the 1 player has activated a pinch, but is no longer on the pinch, because of a pass; the 1 player must cover the elbow.
     - Once the ball goes below the foul-line extended. The 4 player, has the pinch anywhere below foul-line extended. The 4 player is in the middle of the press, but seeks to intercept ball-side passes and pinch ball-side dribbles.
     - Player 5 is in the back of the defense and covers the ball-side block.

- The objective is to stop dibbles and pinch them, and to anticipate and steal passes (Do Not Pinch Passes) - wings stay on their side of the floor and or responsible for the player with the ball when she is on the wing's side of the floor.
- Run transition, if a steal is made. Be quick, be fast, but don't be in a hurry.

- **Covert 4** -

  (Opponents have side take-in on own defense side)

  A. **Main Coaching Points for team** - Set-up in TRAP, TRAP, TRAP; a 1-2-1-1 half court pressure formation. Player 1 lines up at 5 second line, one wing lines-up at the foul-line extended on the right side, the other wing, lines up at the foul-line extended on the left side. Player 4 lines up on the foul-line. Player 5 lines up in the paint, between the blocks.
     - The ball -side wing and player 1 pinch on the dribble
     - The ball-side wing and player 4 pinch on a ball-side pass
     - Weak-side wing covers backside block, when the ball is clearly on the other side of the floor and outside of the red zone
     - Player 5 covers ball-side block
     - Skip pass is covered by wing and player 4 (Key to this tough assignment is for players in the strong side pinch to make the skip pass very difficult to make
     - Play defense by moving feet, keep hands out and away from opponent, do not reach.
     - Run transition, if a steal is made. Be quick, be fast, but not be in a hurry.
     - Main Coaching points for individuals - Same as for team, but also be ready to Run transition, if a steal is made. Be quick, be fast, but not be in a hurry.

Target 5:
(Our team loses offensive rebound)
- **Definition** - When our team misses a shot and loses the rebound
- **Response** - Same as Target 2 - **SCRAMBLE** (Our team gets back fast, in the lane, to defend our goal - Use either a Trap, 23 Zone, or man defense - this will be pre-determined at team, planning)

  Main Coaching Points for the team - Same as Target 2 - **SCRAMBLE** (Our team gets back fast, in the paint, to defend their goal - Use either a Trap, 23 Zone, or man defense - this will be pre-determined at team, planning time)
  A. **Main Coaching Points for the team** - (Get a stop - Retreat back into lane to regroup into a planned response)
  B. **Main Coaching Points for individuals** - Protect the lane first, get at least one foot in the lane before you move to planned defensive response. Do not foul - Look to steal passes not dribbles.
- **Covert 5 -**
  (Our team has side take-in)
  A. **Main Coaching Points for team** - Run Line take-in - player four inbounds the ball - Players 1, 2, and 3 form a straight line facing in-bounder, Player 5 is on ball-side block. Players in the line break in different directions on signal from in-bounder. Once ball is inbounded move to offense position (Offense is pre-decided before the game)
  B. **Main Coaching points for individuals** - Make crisp V-cuts and crisp passes. Don't be in a hurry. Get the ball in then work for a good open shot. Only take your shot. If you get the ball in a place that is not your shot, look to drive or pass. If there is no defensive pressure, player 3 immediately goes to set-up in ball-side corner.

Target 6:
(Our team gets defense rebound)
- **Response - OUTLET to transition**
  - A. **Main Coaching Points for the team** - Player 1 looks to receive OUTLET pass, between 5 second line and foul-line extended.
    - Player 2 JETS (Runs fast) to receive long pass on the run, looking to get a quick layup.
    - Player 3 runs to right baseline corner looking for long pass and possible 3 point shot.
    - Player 4 runs to left baseline corner, looking for a long pass and a possible baseline or middle of paint drive.
    - Player 5 trails the play, as safety, in case of steal, by the opponents. Also, player 5 is the secondary break moving down the middle of the paint for a pass, if the other options were unavailable. Player 5 goes to ball-side block, and rests there until the ball is reversed.
    - Player 1, after she passes the ball, takes a V-cut at the ball-side elbow to receive a pass, to reverse the ball.
    - Player 3 or 4 whomever is away from the ball breaks high to receive the reverse pass.
    - Player 5 cuts to screen for player 1 when the ball is reversed.
    - The player that passed the ball to player 1 cuts across the paint on the baseline to look for a possible pass on the opposite 3 point circle.
    - The player that receives the reverse pass from player 1; looks to shoot or drive first, then looks for the player cutting across the baseline second, then looks for player 1 cutting to the basket third.
    - Once player 5 screens for player 1, she rolls to weak-side block

B. **Main Coaching Points for individuals** - Timing is everything!

- **Covert 6** -

(Jump ball to begin the game)

A. **Main Coaching Points for team** - Player 5 jumps
  - Player 1 straddles the mid-court line to player 1's right hand side.
  - Player 2 straddles the mid-court line to player 1's left hand side.
  - Player 3, faces player 5, on the mid-court circle.
  - Player 4 plays safety on the opponent's foul-line
  - If the opponents get the tip; SCRAMBLE! Get a stop!

B. **Main Coaching points for individuals** - (Use the jump ball as an aggressive offensive play)
  - Player 5 tries to tip the ball to player 3 or 2
  - As the tip is made, Player 1 Jets straight toward the block nearest her.
  - The player that receives the tip throws a "rainbow pass" to Player 1
  - Once the pass is made to player 1 or the tip goes elsewhere (Not to player 3) Player 3 sprints to the weak baseline corner; looking for a long pass and a 3 point shot.
  - Player 5 goes at medium speed down the center of the lane looking for a secondary break pass. No pass then go to the weakside block

Target 7: Our team has take-in under own basket

- **Definition** - Our team has a take-in under our basket
- **Response** - Stack Variations (1, 2, or 3)
- **Practice Time Splits** -
  (Team 7 minutes, Individual, 5 minutes, Covert, 3minutes)
  A. **Main Coaching Points for the team** - Get the ball in and get a good shot
     - Player 4 is the in-bounder
     - Player 3 lines-up on the ball-side block
     - Player 5 lines-up, right behind player 3
     - Player 1 lines-up in the base-line corner on the 3 point circle
     - Player 2 lines-up in the weak-side, base-line corner on the 3 point circle
  B. **Main Coaching Points for individuals** - Same as A.
- **Covert 1** - Our team shoots free throws (Repeat - from Trigger 1)
  A. **Main Coaching Points for team** - Aggressively block out and hustle for the rebound by creating the rebounding triangle; gather rebound, then right back up with the ball, try to get fouled
  B. **Main Coaching points for individuals** - Same as for team, but also be ready to press after we make the basket or be ready to Scramble if the opponents get the rebound

After giving us the big picture of the targets, Coach B told the coaches that they could take notes, about the players during tryouts, on the back of the pages he had given us. Coach B handed each of the coaches and me a clip board. Coach B led us into the gym to meet the players, and to start the competition. Coach B had the parents, of a couple of players, check all the girls in, as they arrived. After players checked in, they were directed, by the parents, to sit along the wall, until everyone was checked in, and the coaches were ready to go.

CHAPTER 8

Basketball Championship Development

The parents organized the tryout. Coach B had worked with the parents, in the previous week, to teach them how to get the players, to the spots they needed to be, once the competition started. First, the players had to be grouped by grade level.

The parents had four lists designated for each grade level. Players lined up to enter the gym. Seniors were told to be first in line, then juniors, then sophomores, then freshmen. As the players moved to the sign-in table, each was signed in, then given a piece of paper with a number. Numbers on the papers were from 1 to 60.

After being signed-in, and receiving a number, players helped each other attach the sheets, on the back of player t-shirts, with safety pins. Each player was told to memorize her number, for the remainder of tryouts. So, it turned out, 55 girls signed-in for tryouts; 10 seniors, 15 juniors, 10 sophomores, and 20 freshmen.

During the first two to three practices, players competed in several events, peculiar to the game of basketball. Players participated in agility, layups, mikan drills, three point shots, and free throws. Players were given an endurance ranking, based on the place finished as compared to the other players. Further, coaches observed players as they competed in one on one, three on three, and four on four games.

The coaches met after the first few practices. Coach B called the first two to three practices, Basketball Camp. After The coaches met to analyze information collected during the camp. Coaches were able to use the information to place players on three official teams; freshman, JV, and the varsity.

The coaches determined, the initial shooting spot assignment for each player (Shots players should practice, and the only shots players should take in a game). Placing players in positions compatible, to the skills of others, on the team, was a focus. Players were also ranked, best to lowest, in terms of shooting, and performance on the skills tests.

Coaches also evaluated the players, overall, in relation to teammates. With this information in mind, coaches placed players on teams one and two, at each level. Coach B saw this evaluation as very important, because it would eventually determine subbing.

Team 1 would most regularly start the game. Team two would be the first subs, at each level. Coach B is a proponent of subbing five players at a time. I asked Coach B about this.

> Coach B said, "I believe players work best as a unit. When players practice, I have them practice as five player teams, therefore, when they are in a game together, they work together, to support each other."

> "Is it wise, to have all your best players off the floor, at the same time?"

> "Maybe this is a big deal to some coaches," Coach B explained, "But I will sacrifice what looks good, or seems right, for something that has so many positives."

"According to Coach B, when team two, enters the game, the team will have a specific mission. This way, team two knows their mission, and the coach will have an opportunity to talk to the team together; easier to make improvements or changes. Also, everyone gets to rest at the same time."

"Exactly what is the mission of team two?"

"Team two's mission is, to give team one a rest, and have more positive stats, during their time played than do the opponents."

"So, what you are saying is that, as long as the opponents do not advance all is good?"

"Yes. For instance, if we are ahead by 5, as team two checks in. We should be 5 or more points ahead when team one checks in again. In this scenario nothing is lost, all is positive."

I thought about what Coach B was saying, and realized once again, that Coach B had a little different way, he looked at things in coaching. As I considered what he was saying, it began to make perfect sense. Players could get fired up; they knew they were all going to play, and play soon, with purpose.

Platoon subbing, as Coach B put it, was a reminder of his football coaching days. It was a great way to keep the players, on team one, rested and hydrated. It was also a good way to keep the players on team two involved, and help them feel vested in the win. Coach B said, within the platoon system, team one, would rarely have to keep playing beyond three minutes straight. Coach B's predetermined playing intervals, were 1.5 to 3 minutes, in and out, for the players, unless they were in, "Broken Arrow."

Coach B told me that "Broken Arrow," was an all-out, man-to-man, full court press. Team one would remain on the floor for two minutes, team two would sub for one minute. Once "Broken Arrow" is initiated, by a coach, and it could only be initiated by a coach, it never stops without the coach saying so.

Practice Progression

I was anxious to see the regular practice routine, but Coach B insisted on, what he called "Slow Cooking." I discovered that "Slow Cooking," was what Coach B initiated, for the first three practices after the, three days of Basketball Camp. During "Slow Cooking" days, was also where the players, on all levels, learned the pre-game routine.

I dropped by practice during the "Slow Cooking" practice days, and noticed that the slower pace, of moving from item to item, was where the big change is. On all three levels the coaches were teaching the techniques of the codes. Instead of reviewing each code every day, the coaches covered just three or four codes for the entire practice.

The three practices, Freshmen Team, JV Team, and Varsity were occurring at the same time and each team was learning the pre-game routine. Coach B wanted players to be able to finish the pre-game in 15 minutes or less. The coaches were expected to insist that the players be precise during each drill.

> Coach B kept repeating loudly so everyone could hear, "Be quick, but don't rush, be precise, but play fast, feet, feet, feet! Keep those feet moving, no walking."

I noticed that the pre-game routine consisted of six activities. I watched as the players of all three teams began practice with a loud team chant (One player would say, "Play Hard!" Everyone else would respond, "All the Time!"), followed by a unifying clap. The players jogged two laps, around half of the floor, in a straight line.

The five drills were taught in specific order; players on each team were divided into two groups. One group made a circle, at the middle circle, and did flexibility exercises, while the other group, shot free throws. Once the group shooting free throws, shot ten free throws, the groups changed places.

Next, the players used four lines, and two balls, to do a layups and passing drill. After the players, shot ten free throws, the next drills were Individual's, Best Shots, Spot drills. After each shooter took 5 shots, players moved to the defense, and drop step drills. Players were placed in two groups. Eight lines and two balls, were used for defense pinch drills, and one ball was used for drop-step drills. The guard and wing players, practiced the pinch and trap; and the slide and turn maneuvers.

Coach B had the players run pregame several times during practice. He wanted them to memorize the sequence. He wanted them to be precise in their movements. He wanted the players, to eventually get to the point, that they could independently, run the pregame, without supervision from coaches.

The real "meat" of the "Slow Cooking" practice days, was having the players learn the codes. The idea was to explain each of the ten codes precisely. These were Coach B's Gestalt practices. He wanted the players to get an overview, big picture, concept of each Code. This he wanted to get accomplished, before practices went into the high speed, rapid response, regular daily routine. The players would get a chance to understand how each code addressed each Trigger.

The coaches would explain the ten codes over three days. The categories for teaching the codes was Tight, Offense, and Spread. On Tight Day, the players learned Scramble, 23, and Bandits. Tight is the scheme to keep the defense compact and stingy around the lane.

On Offense Day, the players learned Outlet, Breaker, Zorro, Free-Throws, Stack, and Double. Offense is the scheme where players were taught to quickly look to score. Players were taught to take all good shots (only shots in their personal shooting spots), layups, and try to get fouled in the act of shooting. Players were also taught the in-bound plays.

On Spread Day, the players learned the Press, the Trap, and Broken Arrow. I learned that the idea behind the Spread scheme, is to make the opponents, have to face obstacles, as they try to matriculate, the ball down the floor. During the Spread component our team seeks to redirect the ball handler, pinch dribblers, and steal passes.

Regular Practice Routine

I noticed, as I visited a few of the regular practices, that every regular practice, begins and ends, with the same routine. Many of the drills were different, but the codes kept everything constant. With only six weeks remaining until the first game, coach B, the assistant coaches, and the players were focused. Each player learned the importance of each code, and the Trigger the codes address.

Tight Component

Players learned that within the Tight component of the system, the codes Scramble, 23, and Bandit's addressed specific Triggers.

The Tight component addresses the Triggers that occur, when our team misses a shot, and loses the rebound, when Opponents' cross midcourt on offense, when Opponents have a side take-in, on their own offense side, when Opponents' have a take-in, under their own basket, and when the Opponents, have a side take-in on their own defense side of the floor.

Offense Component

Within the Offense component of the system, the codes Zorro, Outlet, Stack, Doubles, and Breaker address a large number of Triggers. For example, the Offense codes activate when our team has the ball, on our team's own side of the court, seeking to score. The Offense also activates when our team gets a defensive rebound, when the Opponent shoots free throws, when the Opponent presses, when our team has a take-in, under our own basket, or when our team has a side take-in.

Spread Component

The Spread component of the system has four codes, Swarm, Press, Trap, and Broken Arrow. The codes within the Spread component activate when our team makes a Shot, when the Opponents' cross midcourt on offense, and when the momentum changes toward the opponents, but our team could still win the game.

When I returned to see the last week of practice, before the first game, I could feel the energy and excitement, of the players and the coaches. Each of the regular practices began with the pregame routine. The varsity players had worked the time of the drill completion down to ten minutes. They were proud of themselves because Coach B was impressed.

After the pregame drills the team moved to the drills within the Tight component of the system. Coach B and Gramps were disciplined to stay within the 15 minute limit for each component. Gramps set the game clock to 15 minutes, and the practice began with a team huddle.

> Coach B said, "Seven days remaining. Play hard."

> Everyone on the Varsity Team responded, "all the time!"

The team all clapped in unison. I wasn't even on the team, but I could actually feel the collective resolve as the team broke the huddle. As the huddle broke, the varsity began their team drills in the Tight category. Team 1 started by doing the Swarm drill. Swarm activates when one of the opponents grabs a defensive rebound.

To practice Swarm, both teams were on the floor around the basket. Team 1 started on defense. Team 2 started on offense. Gramps threw the ball in the air, like a jump ball, where the players were standing. All of the players jumped high, but for the sake of the drill, Team 1 players allowed a Team 2 player to catch the ball as it came down.

> As soon as the player caught the ball; Team 1 players yelled, "Swarm, Swarm.

> Team 2 players yelled "Outlet!" Then tried to get the ball across mid-court.

Players 4 and 5 sprinted to pinch the player with the ball. Player 2 and 3 covered the, outlet area nearest, to each of them. On the side that the outlet came out, the Team 2 player receiving the ball, was immediately pinched by the nearest Team 1 Player.

The nearest, to the passed ball, of Player 4 and Player 5, ran to help pinch the ball. The remaining Player of the two players, moved into a deny defensive stance, on the rebounder. As soon as Swarm was called, Player 3 immediately covered the area around the mid-court circle.

The Team 1 player, on the weakside of the floor, moved fast to cover the area, at the top of the key. After Team 1 had a turn practicing Swarm, the teams switched, Then Team 2 was allowed to practice Swarm. Each team practiced Swarm twice.

After practicing Swarm, the teams transitioned into Scramble. Scramble is activated when the opponents, have control of the ball, and are moving toward their own basket in an attempt to score. Scramble is code, that expresses to everyone, to get in the lane fast, to guard against a layup first.

To set-up the drill for Scramble, the players on Team 1 moved around, in a circle, in the lane.

Gramps shouted "Shot!"

All players on the varsity responded, "Block Out!"

All five of the players squatted, feet in a wide stance, facing the basket, arms and hands held high, to receive an imaginary rebound. Gramps took one dribble.

All players on the varsity yelled, "Scramble!"

All of the players on team 1, sprinted to the other end of the court where Coach B was waiting. As they were running, Team 2, stepped onto the floor and duplicated what team 1 had done earlier. When team 1 arrived, at the other end of the floor to touch the "paint in the lane," and turned to face the imaginary fast break, from the imaginary opponent, Coach B was fussing.

"Too slow, you've got to be faster!"

Team 1 immediately took a defensive stance, as the players moved into a 23 defense formation. Coach B faced them and pointed in different directions, directing the players, to do defensive step and slides, left, right, back, then a short sprint forward. Afterward, team 1 sprinted off the floor, to the right side line. They were sprinting, to return to the other end of the court, to start running in a circle again as Gramps waited.

Both teams continued through the drill three times. The drill was perpetual motion. Once the drill started, it seemed to flow, no walking, continuous running, sprinting, agility. The Scramble drill went on, for about 2 to 3 minutes.

After the Scramble drill, Team 1 and Team 2 moved to join Coach B. Team 1 set-up in 23 Defense under the direction of Coach B. Team 2 set-up in a five-out offense. Team 2, under the direction of Gramps, passed the ball, around the perimeter. Each player had to take one dribble before passing. The teams participated in a Shell Drill, with certain coaching points being emphasized.

Coach B focused on the players on offense, moving to the correct positions, in relation to the ball. Special emphasis was placed on footwork, and body positioning. The stances were to be wide, the hands out, protecting against drive attempts (This was just practice, no actual driving attempts, by the offense, just ball movement). The Shell Drill went on for about thirty seconds, Coach B called for a shot. The player with the ball shot.

The team on offense immediately blocked out the nearest player. The team on offense "crashed the boards" to get the rebound. The drill stopped when someone got the rebound. If one of the players on offense got the rebound, the players on defense had to do ten pushups.

The teams switched; Team 2 played the 23 defense, under the direction of Coach B. Team 1 played the five-out offense, under the direction of Gramps. The coaches coached, and the players ran the shell drill. This drill went on for two to three minutes.

After the 23 shell, the Bandits Drill began. The set-up was the same, and the procedure was the same as the 23 Shell. Team 1 was on defense (Man to Man) first. Coach B focused on reminding the players to move their feet; hands out, no reaching, power stepping, and sliding through against the off ball screen.

Coach B reminded players, who were guarding the screener, to warn their partner, by yelling out screen. Coach B also reminded players, who guard the screener, to help by pulling the player being screened through. Although keeping fidelity with the simulation, and not really trying to steal the ball, Coach B continued to remind them.

To keep them thinking, Coach B repeatedly said, **"Stop the dribble, steal the pass!"**

Team 2, from the five-out formation, ran a pass and screen-away offense. Players on offense were not to drive and not to dribble. Gramps watched the offense to make sure, the rules were followed, and that every time a pass was caught, the receiver moved to the triple-threat position, before she made a pass. This part of the Tight component took about two to three minutes.

In all, counting the pregame drill, and the Tight Component drills, including Scramble, 23, and Bandits, took about 27 minutes. The team drills moved to the Offense Component. Team 2 remained with Gramps, under one basket. Team 1 jogged down the floor, to work with Coach B.

Both teams practiced the flow of "Zorro," the offense pattern.

The teams ran through the pattern, twice with Gramps, then twice with Coach B. The players moved from coach to coach, by way of running along the sideline on their right.

Zorro starts with a pass. The pass could go to the ball-side corner, the weak-side corner, or the high post. I watched closely, so I could understand the intricacies of the offense.

Coach B told me, some time ago, that he used only one offense, whether against man or zone. The players just used different options. I drew it on my tablet, as the players went through the options.

It was interesting how, the Offense Component of the system, was practiced in combinations. Again, the players were grouped into two teams. Team 1, remained with Coach B, under the west basket (I watched at Coach B's basket first, then moved to watch Gramps coach), while team 2 moved to the opposite end of the floor with Gramps. Both coaches asked the teams to run through Zorro. I tried to get it written as the teams ran the play.

1. Players 2 and 3 aligned themselves in a corner, opposite each other.
2. Player 5 began on the block, opposite of the ball-side (She would move to high post if Player 1 was having trouble getting the ball to a corner).
3. The point guard (Player 1), started Zorro at mid-court; by passing the ball, to player 2 or player 3 in one of the corners, or to player 5 coming to the high post (Only if the corner players were covered).
4. Player 4 followed about 5 or 6 feet behind Player 1.
5. When Player 1, passed to the ball-side corner, player 1, cut through the lane expecting a pass from the player who received the pass in the corner.

a. If a pass from the corner does not go to player 1, player 1 replaces the player, in the corner opposite the ball

b. If a pass is received by player 1, she should shoot - if she cannot shoot, she should kick the ball to a corner (preferably the weakside corner) or back to player 4, who by that time had moved closer to the top of the key area

6. Once the pass is received by a corner player:

- Receiver of the pass, should come to triple threat position; then look to shoot or drive, depending on her "personal best spot" situation.

- If there is no shot possibility, look for a pass to Player 1, in the paint, or for player 5, coming to the ball-side block after Player 1 cuts through.

- If no pass is available, drive if there is a gap, if there is no gap, kick the ball out to player 4.

- Player in the weak corner sprints to the area above the top of the key extended, and outside of the lane-line extended, looking for a pass from player 4, to reverse the ball.

- Once the ball is reversed, player 4 switches with the player in the weak-side corner. Then everything repeats from the ball-side.

- If Player 5 receives the high post pass, Player 1 may cut off either side, down the lane, looking for a handoff, then rotates to weakside corner. If there is no handoff, Player 5 pivots to face the basket. Looks for the personal best shot option, or passes the ball to either corner.

Again, the teams switched places to hear a different coach talk to them, as they practiced the play. But what was really cool, was that Zorro, was practiced from how it would occur from Outlet,

Breaker, Stack, and Doubles. The objective, of course, according to Coach B's philosophy, is to score quickly. Therefore, the objective of the Offense Component was to score; always, always, to score. Coach B's system, was not designed, to get to a position, to run offense, but rather to be relentless in efforts to score.

A shot should only occur from the shooter's best individual shot area. Each player should only have two best shots (This has to be agreed upon by the coach, and supported by data). Therefore, each player could shoot, either of the two of her best shots. (Additionally, any player may shoot open layups and free throws). Each player will get plenty of opportunities to shoot, if they stay disciplined to this rule. But the team as a whole will always be taking their best shots. Fewer missed shots and more shots attempted. Coach B says, it is just as bad for a player, to pass up an open, personal best shot, as it is selfish, to take a shot outside of their own personal best area.

Team 1 practiced Outlet, by doing the "circle thing" again. The players on team 1 ran around in a circle in the lane. Gramps shot to purposely miss.

- Someone on Team 1, grabbed the rebound (probably player 4 or 5).
- Player 2 (The Jet), immediately sprinted to receive a long pass, looking for a quick layup.
- Player 1, darted immediately to the area, nearest the rebounder, outside the red zone, between the foul-line, and the five second line, looking to receive a pass, from the rebounder, then loudly yells Outlet!
- The rebounder looked to throw, the long pass, to the Jet first, if the Jet is not clearly open, then she passed the ball to the outlet.
- Player 3, sprinted to the weakside corner, on the offense side of the court.

- Player 5, sprinted to the weakside block, on the offense side of the court.
- Player 4, trailed the play.
- Upon receiving the outlet pass, Player 1 looked to pass to the Jet first, then to the near corner, on the other end, to start Zorro.

In the drill, no shot was taken, until the team transitioned into Zorro, and ran it through one time. Once a shot was taken, on Coach B's command, team 1 cleared the floor, to their right, then ran, down the side-line, back up court. While Team 1, was running back up-court, Team 2 ran through the drill. The teams ran through the Outlet drill two times each.

Breaker was run by team 1, while team 2 played a pressing defense. Player 4 did the inbounding. Player 4 tried to inbound the ball to Player 1. Player 2 sprinted to the ball side corner. Player 3 moved to the nearest area, between the top of the key extended to the midcourt line. Player 5 moved to the area inside the midcourt circle. After the inbound pass, player 4, stepped to the area across the lane from Player 1.

Once the ball was inbounded on Breaker; Player 1, looked to get the ball up the floor, to Player 2, 3, or 5. If Player 1, gets the ball to any one, of the players, 2, 3, or 4, Player 1, then sprints to the corner, opposite Player 2. If Player 1 cannot get the ball to any of the three players up the court, Player 1 reverses the ball to Player 4. Player 4 was coached to look, for Player 3 or 5 for a pass. Player 5 makes herself big in the middle, moving in search of a clear pass receiving lane. The concept is that there should be minimal dribbling, during Breaker, but instead almost all passing.

Also, within the Offense Component the players practiced take-ins. For the take-in under, their own basket the teams used the code Doubles. Team 2 practiced with Gramps, while team 1 practiced with Coach B. After about 1 minute the teams switched coaches and practiced Doubles again.

In Doubles, Player 4 inbounded the ball to the open player. As they faced the basket Player 1 occupied the left corner, Player 2 occupied the right corner. Player 3 stepped on the ball-side block facing, Player 4. Player 5 lined up directly behind player 3. There were four options from the stack, and a possible pass or drive or shot after a possible pass from Player 4.

After practicing Doubles, using the same procedure, Teams 1 and 2 practiced Stack. Stack is a formation used for side take-in. Player 3 lines up two to three feet on the court, facing Player 4.

Player 2, lines up just behind Player 3. Player 1 lines up just behind Player 3, and player 5 lines up just behind player 1. The players break opposite directions on the signal from Player 4.

Player 5 waits until all the other players have cut, then Player 5 goes straight to the ball. Player 4 inbounds the ball, looking for Player 1 or Player 2. Once the ball is inbounded, all of the players run to their positions for Zorro.

I was keeping the time, for myself, of how long the drills were taking. When Coach B first started talking to me, some months' ago, about how he would run practices, I thought there would not be enough time, in a regular practice, to drill all of the codes, within every component. However, even after practicing, all of the codes, in two of the components, there was still more than 20 minutes remaining, to cover the Spread Component.

In following the regular procedures, Team 1 practiced "Trap," on one side of the court with Coach B. While Team 2, simultaneously, practiced "Trap" with Gramps at the other end of the court. This occurred for one minute, splits. Each team practiced with each coach for two minutes, for a four minute total.

Press defense practice began with Team 1 playing defense and team 2 playing offense for 1 minute. The teams switched at the end of one minute. Each team had the opportunity, to practice Press twice, to total 4 minutes of practice in the Spread defense area. The same process for practicing Press, was used for practicing "Broken Arrow."

More than ten minutes remained once the coaches were finished with the Spread Component. The remaining ten minutes could be used, to revisit individual drills. Also, the ten minutes could be used to revisit Pregame Drills. Either way, players could have an opportunity to repeat individual skills, they needed to practice.

Later, when talking to Coach B, he told me that the time allotted for Stack, Doubles and individual drills was used to do weight training instead, two days a week. Gramps had convinced Coach B that weight training was essential to keeping the girls' injury free. Gramps explained that most girl's teams probably, never did weight training. Gramps added, that the ones that did do weight training, probably only did it in the off season. Gramps was certain that a consistent weight training program would, along with adding strength, and endurance, would boost confidence.

Coach B had incorporated so much of what I had heard that he and Gramps talked about over time. I could actually identify the interconnection between the Essential Keys (Drilling the Codes, and Cues and Options), and the Six Central Components (Team Expectations, Team Identity, Team System, Triggers and Roles, Position Specifics, and Common Language). I was excited for the games to start so I could see the Coaching Oversight (Practice, game, and strategy plans) in action.

After I watched the first few practices, I realized the Crossroads Crusaders were going to be formidable, once the season started. In my job as a sports reporter, I had seen many girls' basketball teams' practice. I could see that the Crusaders were already, organized and ready to play.

Let the Games Begin

Coach B knew he had to play every team in his conference twice. In the conference were several strong Missouri Class 2 teams. The Crusaders had to face, Crystal City, Bismarck, Transportation and Law, Valley, Viburnum, and Summerville. Conference play would account for ten games, and Coach B wanted the team, to have played, twenty games by playoff time. Coach B wanted to schedule ten non-conference games, perhaps two tournaments.

Coach B was certain the Crusaders would make it to the playoffs, and maybe go as far as, the Sweet Sixteen. However, Coach B never expressed these aspirations, outside of private conversations, between him, his staff, and me. Since this would be the first varsity season for Crossroads, in the history of the school, Coach B knew that none of the other coaches, expected the Crusaders to be a challenge this season.

Coach B had scheduled the first game with Principia High School, a team out of the same district, but not in the same conference. Principia had a solid team, but had not been a real threat in the St. Louis area, or in Division 2 over all. Coach B said that he was anxious, to see how the Crusaders would do, during a real game, running what Coach B called his, Piranha System.

Coach B had lined-up a tough non-conference schedule. Coach B had it so that he would play all higher class teams in the rest of the non-conference schedule. He even had two games scheduled with out of town teams. Coach B wanted to build his competition level so that the players would not be intimidated, by the time they got to the playoffs.

Finally, the evening of the first varsity game was upon us. I had work, so I missed the J.V. game that was played first. Some of the JV players saw me enter the gym, after their game, while the varsity was doing pregame, and ran over to me, all excited. They won their game 45 - 27. I was very happy for them. Katy was all smiles.

The game was an away game for the Crusaders, I knew that could be intimidating, especially for the first game. I could sense, even from the bleachers, that the varsity girls, and the coaches seemed nervous. This game would be the first test of Coach B's system. It was very exciting for me to watch them going through their pre-game drills, getting ready to play.

I could hear Coach B's final words to the team, before they took the floor. It was the same thing that he said to them to start practice, so many weeks prior. It was the same thing, he said to them between drills at practice. It was the last thing, he said to them, at the end of practice. Now, it was the last thing he said to them, before they took the floor, for the jump ball, of their very first game of the season.

Coach B said, "Play hard!"

"All the time." The players responded.

Everyone with their hands touching in the center of the circle said, "Gooo, Crossroads!" Followed by a very snappy clap.

That simple, pre-jump ball ritual, seemed to calm everyone. However, my nervousness, had not disappeared completely. After having followed them until this point, I felt like I was part of the team too. I could sense, the coaches and players were fired up and ready to go.

Cassidy Allen, the 6'1" center jogged out to do the jump ball, to start the game. The rest of the team, sprinted to their places for the start of the game. 5'10 strong forward, Maggie Dupree, waited, as a safety, in the lane, on the defensive side of the floor. 5'9" shooting forward, Brooke Donovan, straddled the middle line, outside the circle, facing Cassidy. Coco Steward, 5'6" shooting guard, stood on the opposite side of the middle circle, facing Brooke. Point guard, 5'4" Destiny West, stood right outside of the middle circle with her back to the offense basket.

The objective of the jump ball play is for Cassidy to get the ball to Destiny. Then Destiny was to pivot toward Coco, then toss a rainbow pass, as Destiny ran an arc pattern toward the basket for a layup. I had watched the team practice that play, I know, at least 50 times. The Play worked perfectly. Bam! The Crusaders jumped out in front, 2-0.

It was an exciting game; in that it was the first game of the season. The Crusaders, scored first and never looked back. The players were tenacious as they smothered the offensive attempts, of the Principia Panthers, with a massive defensive attack. It seemed like the Crusaders were intercepting almost every pass, then transitioning them into, Fastbreak layups. I thought, the Crusaders would be good, but the display they unleashed, had to be a shocker to the Panthers.

The season continued much like the first game. The Crusaders lost only twice. Both times they lost, it was to teams above their class. Teams in Class 4 and class 5 have many advantages over class 2 teams, which probably partially explained the defeats. Nevertheless, the Crusaders made it to the Sweet Sixteen as Coach

B predicted. However, they did not stop there. The Crusaders, moved on to win at the Elite Eight. They did not stop there. The crusaders marched into the final four and eventually won the class 2 State Championship. Coach B's Piranha System works.

Coach B's team, a first year varsity team, with a staff that was new to the players, and new to the school, won the conference championship, won the district championship, and won the state championship. I was excited to be writing the book about Coach B. However, Coach B's story, is about more than winning the state championship. It is a story about meeting challenge with tenacity, leadership, character, honor, and about believing in yourself. Everyone could learn a few things from Coach B's story.

Printed in the United States
by Baker & Taylor Publisher Services